PENGUIN B
DANGERL

Eunice de Souza taught English literature at St. Xaviers College, Bombay for over thirty years and retired as Head of the English Department. Her published works include four books of poems and books for children. Her poems have been translated into Portuguese, Italian and Finnish. This is her first novel.

Eunice de Souza lives in Bombay.

DANGERLOK

Eunice de Souza

PENGUIN BOOKS

Penguin Books India (P) Ltd., 11 Community Centre, Panchsheel Park, New Delhi 110 017, India
Penguin Books Ltd., 80 Strand, London WC2R 0RL
Penguin Putnam Inc., 375 Hudson Street, New York, NY 10014, USA
Penguin Books Australia Ltd., Ringwood, Victoria, Australia
Penguin Books Canada Ltd., 10 Alcorn Avenue, Suite 300, Toronto, Ontario, M4V 3B2, Canada
Penguin Books (NZ) Ltd., Cnr Rosedale & Airborne Roads, Albany, Auckland, New Zealand

Copyright © Eunice de Souza 2001

All rights reserved

10 9 8 7 6 5 4 3 2 1

Typeset in Nebraska by Sakshi DTP Option, Delhi
Printed at Saurab Print-O-Pack, Noida.

This book is sold subject to the condition that it shall not, by way of trade or otherwise, be lent, resold, hired out, or otherwise circulated without the publisher's prior written consent in any form of binding or cover other than that in which it is published and without a similar condition including this condition being imposed on the subsequent purchaser and without limiting the rights under copyright reserved above, no part of this publication may be reproduced, stored in or introduced into a retrieval system, or transmitted in any form or by any means (electronic, mechanical, photocopying, recording or otherwise), without the prior written permission of both the copyright owner and the above-mentioned publisher of this book.

For Margaret D'Souza,
Inspired teacher, generous friend,
and for Anjali Lokur

Acknowledgements

Thanks to Melanie Silgardo and Rebecca Swift for reading the manuscript.

Dear David,

You can't imagine the trouble I had getting the last letter off to you. I went to the usual Post Office down the road but the lady who sells stamps said she was just leaving, her husband wasn't well, and I should go to the Post Office further down.

There was a little gnome of a man sitting there with what looked like minus ten glasses. I gave him my letters and he held them near his nose for some time and then said, I can't give you so many stamps, what will I give the other customers? I told him I was second in the queue and how could he not have stamps, and anyway I would have to take a rickshaw to the next Post Office, and the skunk says, What to do, tell the government. I'll report you, I said, though I had no idea where or to whom, but I was beginning to feel a bit screechy.

The stamps appeared, but he had his little victory anyway. He refused to frank them after I had gummed the stamps down with the messy paste provided. He said I should put them straight in the box in front of his window. I told him someone would steal the stamps, and he said, How can they, I can see the box, can't I? I went home and made myself a very strong mug of tea. I told the bai all about it. Dangerlok, she says, all dangerlok. It's a word she's made up and covers all occasions. Dangerous people, tiresome people, people she doesn't like. Dangerlok.

Love,
Rina

December, and smog hangs low over the city. It is a relief, as the train trundles into Charni Road station, to catch a glimpse of the sea, between tall buildings and casuarina trees.

Civilization, she thinks. It's an old joke: anyone who lives in South Bombay thinks the world begins and ends at Churchgate, then there are just some hamlets beyond.

There's sudden activity. The *Times* is folded and put away, others catching up on sleep jolt themselves awake. Then there's a rush to catch a bus or share a taxi, and oh dear, another new day has begun.

It's difficult to read on the train, it shakes and rattles along. The walls of the compartment are covered with graffiti, randy schoolboy drawings of gigantic genitals scratched into the paint. Rakesh loves Sheela. Nor are overheard conversations always very interesting. Bosses, it would seem, are uniformly a pain in the neck and every other joint as well. Perched on half a seat called the fourth seat, Rina refreshes her lipstick, pats her hair, picks up her books and makes for the door.

I could have done so many things, I could have realized so many dreams if weariness, an inconceivable, enormous weariness had not overpowered me for the last fifteen years or so, or even far longer. A weariness that kept me from working but also from resting, from enjoying life and being happy and relaxing, and also kept me from turning more towards others, as I'd have wished to...oh, if that 'what's the use?' had not germinated in my soul...

Ionesco, Fragments of a Journal

Rina reads the Ionesco passage with her class and says, Tell me, do you ever feel the way he does; what's the use? Rahi's hand shoots up. When I attend FC class, she says. The class laughs in sympathy.

Okay, that's something you consider useless. How about when you feel you're doing something useful? Like teaching steet children, as some of you do.

Bini says, energetically, Well I teach street children, and I often think what's the use. I sometimes scold them, but they don't get their homework done. It's really frustrating.

She pauses uncertainly as the class cracks up.

It's okay, Bini, she says, they're laughing because you've just recited the story of my life. But, she goes on. Suppose they did do their homework and you were happy with them. Would you still ask what's the use?

Carl says, Yes. It's a drop in the ocean.

Okay, so now let's look at what Ionesco may have meant.

What, says Carl who appears in the staffroom after class, happens to those who don't believe anything? How do they know what's right or wrong? Aren't they frightened of what it's all about? I'm a believer, so at least I know Jesus Christ was definitely around.

She hesitates. There are people who wonder about that, Carl. But it doesn't matter in a way. His life still has meaning for us, don't you think?

Come in and chat whenever you want to, Carl, all right?

He says he will.

Rina is glad Carl has dropped in. Since David left three years ago there haven't been many people she spent time talking to about everything under the sun.

Christmas week Rina discovered a circulating library in her tacky lane. She picked up a book (three rupees a throw), and then walked up the slight incline to the little Post Office which was always out of stamps. What to do said the smiling clerk and she agreed. Then to the cigarette kiosk which was cheaper than the other cigarette kiosks, and stocked lighters as well. She chose a bright blue translucent one and held it up to see that it was full. She had a heap of translucent plastic lighters in bright green, pink and yellow. She curled up on the sofa to read all about energetic fellows who rasped, growled, snapped, snarled and bared their teeth. She took out a cigarette and her blue lighter. Snap. She tried to bare her teeth.

She brewed herself a mug of jungli tea: water, milk, tea leaves all bunged in together till they came to the boil. She sat on the sofa with her hands cupping the warm mug, but she waited a minute or so for the tea to be less than scalding. Sometimes she and the bai would have tea together. Sugar to taste. Two spoons and a bit for her. Three for the bai. Less than a year from now they would sit like this, on a morning with a nip in the air, their hands around their mugs of tea. The bai would tell her what the dangerlok had done to the other dangerlok. Ali had sold what was left of his wrecked bicycles and moved who knows where. The mutton man repaired his shop, which was made of corrugated sheeting. They had only been able to wrench out the door. Sometimes there was a little goat tied to this door, twitching its perky tail. She would look the other way.

This must have been the day after Babri and before the bombs. Before the bombs probably. Like so many others, she must have stayed at home, uneasy. The day after Babri she had a seminar in college which finished around three. She walked out to the main road to find it cordoned off. She'd have to walk a bit to find a taxi or a bus to take her to the station for the long commute home. Why is the road cordoned off, she asked indifferently. Another VIP she thought. The stranger shrugged his shoulders and said, Trouble.

A friend in another part of Bombay rang her. Her in-laws, she said, had heard the Muslims were coming by sea. They and other worthies would be ready for them on the terrace, rocks in hands. She did not ask the friend where the in-laws would find the rocks. Her friend did not like her in-laws. Feed them to the Muslims, she said to her friend.

In college she ran into one of the lecturers who she thought was a prick. I saw a photograph of you climbing the Babri dome, she said. He was not amused. She didn't intend him to be. He was a prick. Once he had waved his arms to encompass the college and its trendy undergraduates and asked what was Indian about the place. She had lost her cool. Was picking one's nose Indian? Was listening to Gangubai Hangal Indian? Just walk out of this gate, he had said loftily, you will find India. She had wanted to kick his shins. How many shins can you kick said the lecturer in French who had problems of her own.

Actually, she thought she should have said, my lover is a Muslim. Or one of them is. Heh. Heh. Heh. Not much of a lover and not much of a Muslim. If he suddenly talked about how well Muslims actually treat their women you thought it was just him being quirky and let it pass, or fixed another vodka. She made herself her jungli tea and lit a cigarette. Really it was so peaceful without lovers of any kind, she wondered why she hadn't thought of it before. She always asked after his wife on the phone. Bring her over, she'd say. I've never met her. And the vodka will look like a glass of water with a little ice in it.

Rina's neighbour on the ground floor was from what a BBC newscaster called Utter Pradesh. It was pretty utter, if you dicounted Bihar, which was about as utter as you could get. She owned a few buffaloes, which were kept on a dry spot of land in the swamp next door, next to the really big buffalo shed owned by another Utter Pradeshi. Rina practised her Bombay Hindi on her neighbour and hoped to pick up a shudh phrase or two. Utter would sit in her doorway peeling vegetables. The old mother-in-law in her shabby, faded cotton sari, smoking her bidi, would smile. For many months, Utter would just stare.

Each morning Utter's young sister-in-law would come out with a heap of wet clothes and hang them to dry on the line, which stretched from the pipal tree to their one front window. Each morning the old lady would perform her puja under the pipal tree, drink a mug of steaming tea, smoke her bidi on the outside step. Later she would go inside and come out with the day's litter which she threw on the dry patch of grass in front of their door. There it would lie after the crows and stray dogs inspected it for pickings. Sometimes it would just lie there.

As she walks in through the compound gate, she sees Utter on her front doorstep peeling vegetables.

As she passes, Utter says to no one in particular, That's her boss.

Boss? She is not sure the words are addressed to her. Maybe someone inside the flat.

The girl on the first floor. Her boss.

The girl on the first floor?

She's a kept woman. That's her boss.

Oh! She turns to see a short, podgy man disappearing through the gate.

Mr Chopra, the girl's neighbour, wants her out.

Why?

He says she's a bad girl. He does not want to live near a bad girl. She has nice clothes, she adds. At least six hundred rupees for each salwar-kameez.

Oh!

More than you can afford, says Utter, and smiles.

It will be months before she sees the kept woman. Mr Chopra's petition to the secretary gets no answer.

(When men learn to be men maybe they can handle dames. Mickey Spillane.)

Rina wonders what Utter made of David who came to stay for a few weeks before he went abroad. David says she always stared stonily at him till he began to stare stonily back. She wonders what Utter makes of Jay who brings his car to a halt just outside Utter's door and then yells Hi as Rina watches the little drama from the window.

If Rina ever gets to know, it will be through the

bai who works in several homes, and carries gossip from one to the other.

Dear David,

Guess what! It looks as if all of us on the Board of English Studies will be in jail soon. Some journalist whose name I have never heard of wrote to the police who wrote to the Vice Chancellor who wrote to the Board of Studies to say that there are some obscene words in Arvind's anthology in Arun's poems, and that we are corrupting youth and should be prosecuted. (Did I corrupt you, sweetness?)

Some of the members of the Board have composed a long letter explaining the Nature and Function of Literature, and given it to the Vice Chancellor to give to the police. I don't know what's going to happen.

Had lunch with your mum yesterday. We spent most of the time talking about you.

By the way, don't ring on the weekend of the 27th. I may go to Poona to see an old friend of my mother's who isn't very well. Did I ever mention her to you?

I'm glad the courses are going well and that you

really like New York. Don't be so depressed about not writing these days. How can you with so much course work?

I'll write again soon. I must stop phoning. The last bill was catastrophic.

Love Love

She usually wrote her Christmas letters after Christmas. What was there to say really if one wrote after a year. Dear Dr Walsh, Dear Mrs Mason, How are you? Are you well? I'm well. Fascism is alive and well.

Nothing much happened to her these days. She took a bus to the station and then a train into town, and then another bus, six days of the week. Mondays and Saturdays were the worst, three lectures in a row. It wasn't the classes really. Once inside the classroom, she was more herself than at any other time. They expected something, and she wanted to give it to them. It's a waste of time teaching literature to the young, a writer had once said to her. Not true. Not always true.

Then she came home and flopped on the cane mat (it was cooler than the bed) and turned on the air-conditioner, and read an undemanding novel or napped. With the medication, everything was at one remove. One had to be at one remove or one would go mad, or madder, depending on your point of view. What to do about Ashok, the bright-eyed boy from the slums who paid everyone's electricity and telephone bills for a small sum, till his eyes got brighter and brighter, the voices in his head louder and louder, and now she says Ashok don't you remember me and he just goes by.

The new bus was a great event, coming from the station, crossing the highway, coming down the tacky lane, and back again. The first day it was festooned with flowers, and the driver honked incessantly. Everybody stood at their doors and windows and cheered. A special stop at Queen's Diamonds. Well, special stops everywhere, as the old girl waddled out of her compound gate at the last minute and yelled to the driver to stop.

She always hoped to get the very first seat in the bus, a single one, so she wasn't too near anyone's damp midriff, especially in the summer. The stainless steel vessels (hardly anyone seemed to use brass anymore) were always impeccable. So were the little schoolchildren, with their hair oiled and tightly plaited, and their perky red bows. And the two- and three-year-old idlers, squatting by the roadside, heads bent with interest and satisfaction to watch their little shitties make patterns in the dust.

You mean buses come this way? the taxi drivers would say, as they dropped her at Queen's Diamonds when the arthritis in her knees was playing up. And they made rude comments about the double-parked autorickshaws, the asinine publeek which walked as if it was their father's road, and the governments of the country, both past and present.

You live here? they'd say.

No, I'm visiting my grandmother.

Whenever a new shop opens in the lane she visits it, to encourage it she says. Utter's brother-in-law is lucky, or sensible. He opens the first chemist shop in the lane. With a doctor to the right and another opposite, Queen's Diamonds Chemist Shop will not lack customers. Utter had come with an invitation, and handed it over, unsmiling. She skips the opening but goes later to buy a strip of Aspirin, which she doesn't need. The owner of the circulating library is giving up on James Hadley Chase. He is now into oddments, tubes of gum, ballpoint pens. Gold Spot, and the new extra large plastic bottles of Limca, Coke, Pepsi. He also takes in ironing. She buys herself two ballpoints, one red, one blue. She is beginning to feel proprietorial about this lane, and wishes it well.

The bai says they celebrated Christmas in the slum. Hindi film music and English dance. She enjoyed. Her daughters enjoyed. They celebrate everything: Holi, Ganesh, Gauri, Navratri, Divali, Durga, kite-flying. They are always in debt.

She is also going to rebuild her room, which is really a shanty at the moment.

Oh!

Her daughter is now fourteen and the young men have begun...

The bai divides the world into people who are educated and those who are not. It is normal for those who cannot read and write to have drunken husbands who beat them, and thin daal for dinner. But, she says, today Meera was crying, and she is an educated woman. She says with awe, even educated people cry.

Rina would like to tell the bai about educated people but does not know where to begin.

Anyway, the bai says, I told Meera to pray to Don Boss. I always went to pray to Don Boss before I got married.

Don Boss? Rina suddenly realizes the bai means

the church of St. Don Bosco, fancy church full of marble in some part of Bombay. Ah! Yes, she says, Don Boss.

The bai is radiant. Utter's son, she says, has been hit on the head with a cricket bat. He is a bully who makes off with the balls that come over the wall into Queen's Diamonds from the next compound. He tells the boys there they have no business playing in that compound, the land belongs to his family. It does not. He has been at it again and one of the boys has crept up and hit him on the head, not too hard, just enough for a few sitches. There is a secret rejoicing in Queen's Diamonds.

Rina returns one afternoon to find Utter roaring like a lion, and the other ladies roaring with her. She hangs around to find out what it is all about. The sneaky secretary has been paid vast sums, no doubt about it, to divert water to an unauthorised building next door. There's been hardly any water in the taps all day, and yesterday.

Utter throws her head back and yells oaths and imprecations at the fourth floor where the secretary's wife lurks behind a curtain. Come down mister, she yells at the secretary who is no doubt lurking with the wife. Tell us where you got your new red Maruti car.

A prankster calls the police to say some terrorists have arrived, and in no time a jeep screeches to a halt, with four burly armed men in it. Luckily for the prankster, some ineffective fellow has been pretending he is from the municipal corporation, and the diverting of water is all right. There is no doubt in anyone's minds where he came from. The police haul him off, protesting.

On uneventful days, she, like the other ladies in the building, sits at her window. It's pleasant to watch, as the sun goes down, bright green parrots shriek across the sky.

Her parrots are asleep, perched on a rod in the kitchen.

Sometimes there's an invitation to a seminar out of town and that is a plesant change, especially with the organizers paying for everything. This one is a seminar on Indian poets and several have been invited. She reads the programme note. A presides. B introduces. C speaks. D inaugurates. This is like an EFL lesson. She notices her name is spelt wrong and she mentions it to the chief organizer. He is miffed. He says, That's the schoolteacher in you coming out, and she says, It's nothing to do with teaching, there's a way I spell my name. She thinks, that's the last time I get invited here.

The poets are predictable. Most of them can barely write a line that is alive. She thinks, our naivete is touching. Someone has only to publish something and he or she becomes not just a poet but an eminent poet, and if one can keep up the bluff long enough, the doyen of literature, one of a galaxy of stars who have scaled pinnacles never soared before. She thinks, this is too easy to parody, and tunes in for a minute while a gay poet who is certainly gay but not a poet talks about (oh dear) subversion. She just wishes he could write. She just wishes he didn't feel he had to be subversive every second of the day. Every conversation she overhears runs like this: We must piss on their ideas, we must shit on their ideas, her ideas come from her vagina, etc. He is miffed too because she does not respond to his performance. After she makes a few brief points in an In Conversation session, he says loudly to the audience, Is that a Goan accent? She ignores him. The alternative would be to kick him. How's that, she thinks, for subversion.

She continues to sit in the auditorium. It's air-cooled at least, and outside it's forty-one in the shade.

As she goes down the station stairs to the platform, she hears a loud and raucous burst of music on the public address system. Commuters look at one another and click their tongues. What with the heat, the crowds and the noise they are all going to kill each other one of these days. She can't quite make out the message that follows the music. There are loud crackling sounds on the system. It would appear from what the fellow is saying that one should not trust strangers with one's belongings, and also not accept anything from them, especially food or drink as they may be full of sedatives. (One charming young man has been approaching elderly couples on long-distance trains and offering them sedatives in coffee and then robbing them.) In case of need one should approach the Station Master. What, she thinks, if the Station Master is sedated too? She begins to giggle, and then rummages in her handbag so that the commuters standing next to her do not think she is a lunatic.

When she enters the ladies compartment she is greeted with another sample of concern. Please offer seat to your fellow passengers. They too are human beings. Well, she has no intention of offering a seat. At the most if someone says move, shift, please move, she will wiggle a bit in compliance and continue to sit exactly where she is. It's an old trick she learned travelling second class in the bad old days.

Dear David,

I whizzed down to Poona for two days and spent most of the time walking up and down M.G. Road with the rest of the population. Didn't see a soul I knew. Weird. Every day seems twice as long there and in no time I was dying to get back to filthy smog-ridden, overcrowded Bombay.

I've decided to treat myself to a first class pass. Can't take too much of nature, red in tooth and etc. The other day I was so tired of standing, and the smell of fish, and guavas, and undeodorized armpits, I pinched a woman who pinched the seat I was about to get, and she pinched right back. The first class is emptyish in the afternoons, so I munch Pringles and contemplate the universe.

No, I will not re-work my thesis, I prefer to mope. I don't think I can get back to that stuff again. Every time I see the word Indianness I think yawn yawn. There was another article on the subject in last Sunday's paper. The box said something about non-resident Indian non-resident writers or some such crap.

I think Akhil teaches at Columbia. I don't have an address, but if you contact him say I said. Jay is as ever. I know. I know.

Love, Love

Sometimes Rina and her friend Vera and Vera's husband Mulk and his friend Jay go to the Yacht Club for a drink, or sail across the bay to Mandhwa, or take off for one of the hill-stations close to Bombay. She likes that. She has never been among people who can just take off. See you when I see you.

Rina has never really heard male talk in her life, at least not the kind she hears from Mulk and Jay and their friends who sometimes join them at the bar. She's never heard a man talk about a woman they know and say, laughingly, by now she has cobwebs between her legs. And of course they talk about stocks and shares, yachts, cars, food, cricket. She rarely says much. Sometimes she thinks all she can talk about is Jane Austen, though Jane Austen did know what happened to women with cobwebs between their legs even if she may not have put things in quite that way.

'She was exotically beautiful in the South American manner. Her skin was pale and lovely; her eyes were sultry behind the blue mascara; her scarlet lips promised passion and scorn.' She puts the book down and dials Jay's number.

Jay, will you stay with me forever if I promise you passion and scorn?

Mad or what, says Jay, and puts down the phone.

Rina passes the joint. It is much too acrid. They are on Jay's terrace, looking at a fat gold moon.

I wish I had never come back, he says. I was perfectly happy working in Dunkin Donuts. Save money. Take off. I even went to Peru.

Why don't you go back?

Have you seen the bald spot in the middle of my hair? What are the babes going to think of it?

The babes are not going to think about you, she says. You're stuck with me, unless your memsahib takes you back.

Woman wailing for her demon lover? says Vera. Ever heard of feminism?

No, she says irritated because Vera has made this remark for the third time.

And adds, So why don't you leave your in-laws? You're always grumbling about them.

Why leave a smoothly running flat for some sump in the name of independence? says Vera.

So there you are, she says.

What ideas do you have about feminists? she asks her students, deciding to shoot the first one who says 'strident'. No, of course your father is a nice man. Of course you can wear jewellery. Yes, of course bra burning, but it was a gesture, not the whole caboodle. Don't hesitate to send me an invitation for your wedding.

The taxi drivers and shopkeepers address her as Aunty. All women of a certain age are addressed as Aunty. Actually, there are no women here. All are ladies or ledis. She cannot remember when she graduated from Sister to Aunty, and now the occasional fellow says Maji. The grey is showing in her hair. Sometimes they mistake Vera for her daughter. This annoys her and amuses Vera. Even the hairdresser says, Your daughter hasn't come here for a while. She says mmm and flips through a magazine. She will revenge herself on Vera by reminding her about the embroidery she did and displayed when Mulk came to assess her as a potential wife. There is one stiff rose done in cross stitch, with a brown stem and an unyielding leaf. There is also a pair of bunnies on a pillowcase, very thin bunnies, done in chain stitch. And a green and yellow bead purse with plastic beads. How come Mulk didn't run a mile? she will say. She is amazed to find people still embroider pillowcases (Vera is younger than she is). She thought it went out with her mother's generation.

Vera teaches with her, though a different discipline. They find the same people amusing. Lily Languish drifts in late in the morning, eats a dosa, has a cup of tea, reads the newspaper, has a nap, and leaves. It's possible she has some classes. No one has ever seen her in them.

You mean that's news to you, says one of the cynics at the opposite end of the staffroom. Where have you been? She spends a lot of time with the cynics. They always seem to know what is going on, which teacher takes off on Saturdays, who never turns up to invigilate exams. As a Hindi film poster says, This is the world, and they take it with a cup of tea.

Several, actually.

Rina reads an article which says that Reverend Mother is a hundred that day, Reverend Mother who with her sister founded the college for women she went to in Bombay. The other nuns tell her 'possibly for the hundredth time' that she is going to be a hundred. Is she looking forward to it? Why should I, she says, will I look any better at hundred?

She was possibly, the article goes on, one of the first educationists to introduce sex education for the final year students to 'teach them how to behave with boys and keep their purity'.

She laughs. She remembers those sex education sessions. Reverend Mother sitting at the end of a long corridor, near the nuns' quarters. It is late in the evening, and there is an over-bright lamp on the table. Reverend Mother's face is in shadow, which is just as well, the girls are in awe of her.

Do you know the difference between a man's body and a woman's?

Maybe they did, maybe they didn't, it all depended. A brave and futile question. How many girls in 1959 would say anything but no?

No, Reverend Mother.

Reverend Mother sighs, draws what in that over-bright light looks like a vague and wavy line.

Do you understand?

Oh yes, Reverend Mother.

My dear, one of the nuns had said to her in the kindest way possible in her last year of college, you must marry or become a nun, otherwise you will be lonely when you are old, and there will be no one to look after you.

Well, options had widened since then. She could have gone to the Gulf and made a lot of money. Or she could keep parrots. Or sit quietly at home and read detective stories. Not spy stories. Most self-respecting spies were angst-ridden these days, and she did not want to complicate her emotions. She has had enough debacles. Same saga, different names, as her friend Vera would say, briefly and brutally. Then they'd giggle.

It's a pity she did not keep parrots in her earlier and more impressionable days. She would have learned a thing or two. She watches the female look adoringly at the male, stretch herself flat out in inviting positions on the curtain rod. The male goes on wrecking lighters or toothbrushes or whatever has taken his fancy at the time. Sometimes she gets fed up and nips his tail or a claw.

Le saga Julian. Waifs and strays, he had said. We are both waifs and strays. Thus Julian, fleeing from navy brass and three years in Cambridge. She had a teaching job and he was VSOing in India. His parents said, if you insist on marrying you would have to go and live in Brazil where they don't mind about these things. Think of the children. She hadn't wanted children anyway, but Julian did.

No, she had not kept her silk brocade wedding sari. She exchanged it one day for two stainless steel containers with the woman who trades in these things for old clothes. She still has the stainless containers, one for sugar and one for tea. It wasn't too bad a bargain, the silk had developed brown spots from being unused, and where can one go in

Bombay in silk brocade anyway, too corny.

The containers are on a shelf in the kitchen within easy reach, and every day she bungs in the tea and the milk and water and two spoons of sugar and makes her jungli tea, and smokes six cigarettes per mug. After that she is ready for the day.

Years after the Julian debacle she had been invited, one day out of the blue, to a reception on the HMS Invincible which was docking in Bombay. She couldn't think who had invited her or why but went along anyway. Chatting with an officer she said, I've lost track of Admiral so and so whose son was a friend of mine. Do you think you could locate his address for me? We're sailing to Singapore, the officer said, but I'll find out somehow. And he did. So she wrote to Julian who said why don't you come here and spend a bit of time in Devon. So she went, and smoked in her room while he pottered in the garden or took the children to dance lessons, swimming lessons and other lessons. But they'd go out for dinner in the evenings and drink lots of white wine. They went to meet his friend Andrew who was delighted and said maybe the two of you can get together again (Julian's wife had left him for another). Andrew is a real romantic, and she thinks it would make a good story but no. Julian says, you're not really telling me anything about yourself, and she says, Really there isn't anything to say, just college and one or two dumb relationships, which don't mean anything. Andrew tells her there is a girlfriend who trails in and out, a hard frizzy blonde, and she thinks blonde maybe but definitely not hard and frizzy, it's not Julian's style. And of course Gillian is warm and beautiful, also scatty and extravagant, and she has the most beautiful child she has ever seen. Gillian says, Do you have children, and she says No, I'm not married and Gillian laughs and Julian says You don't have to be married to have children and she says Oh and feels she is a real country bumpkin, but not the Devon kind.

Never mind, she says to Julian, you were only twenty-two, when he says sometimes he still feels like punching his mother's face for the things she said and did. They go to visit his parents who are very polite, and his father says, Julian tells me you are a don and don is a very grand word but still she says, Yes, I'm a don. When they leave Julian says, Don't let them fool you, they are still racist as ever, and she says, Really it doesn't matter, it was all so long ago.

In a way Julian is still '60s', he is a careless dresser, and his children call him by his name, but most of all he doesn't really want to get anywhere. He is happy working on his house (he taught himself building), and in his garden, and teaching a little. And he can still get angry about many things and say so. She finds it difficult to be angry for long, she gets depressed instead, so that everything is at one remove.

Dear David

It was just one of those days. I was reading in the univ library when an elderly gent who works at another table toddled up to me. He asked what I was working on so I told him. Then he says, Your good name? And I told him. Rina Ferreira. Oh! he says, I thought you were an Indian. I didn't know what to say for a moment and then I said, Well I'm not from the moon. I felt a bit bad later for being rude. He wasn't trying to be offensive.

Anyway, the next thing was that that creep Sandeep who is in town wanted to meet me so I said the univ lib so I could get back to work. He came half an hour late and then said let's go and get something to eat. So I said okay. We went to Sundance and he ordered a number of things (luckily the waiter said there was no beer), and when the bill came he said he had to go to the loo. It's years since I've heard that one. Anyway, his hand went in slow motion towards his wallet, but I was so irritated by then I said never mind, I'll get it, and he says, Are you sure? Vera says I should have called his bluff. He's taken some contact numbers, I better warn them.

As I said, it was one of those days. Hope your work is going well.

Love

Really, all this chatter about who is true-blue Indian and who is 'alienated by definition'. Rina had once come across, in the South somewhere, a shop called Lord Tirupathi Chicken House and thought if the owner had no difficulty reconciling Lord Tirupathi with chickens, why should anyone else have a seizure. Rina's very first memories are of riding on an elephant (her father was posted in the tribal areas of Chhattisgarh at the time), and she hopes that is Indian enough! Anyway, she knows who she is. She is a lapsed Catholic who prays in moments of panic, a vague lefty who likes the occasional good meal in a restaurant and does not feel too much guilt about it, a teacher who likes her students and her work but likes the occasional day at home alone. Anyway, it's the writers they are really after, those who write in English. Apparently, one cannot capture the soul of a nation in English. Well, she is not a writer but if she were she would not want to capture the soul of a nation. She would just natter, maybe about parrots or people or a stray pup she had taken to. Does anyone know anything with any clarity about souls or nations? Why does everyone always want to sound more Catholic than the Pope or more Hindu than Lord Tirupathi if it came to that.

Some Cathlics now tag on their ancestral surnames. Lobo-Prabhu or some such, which is fine but she doesn't want to, they can take her or leave her and if mostly they leave her she will not feel—another lovely find in the South on an abandoned railway carriage—'ABONDONED'.

Dear David,

I feel so bored sometimes with the academic scene, or at least the postcolonial part or it. We had a Board meeting today, and a couple of people wanted to make Postcolonialism, Ideology and etc. a core and not an optional course. Luckily, some of the others agreed when I said that hardly anyone seemed to be reading any more, just using texts to ride a hobby horse. What is really irritating is the high moral tone that often accompanies this, always more Catholic than the Pope as we say in these parts, as if we are the first enlightened century and nobody ever asked any questions before. Graham Greene set a novel in West Africa but did not write about blacks but about whites in Africa. Maybe if the woman concerned stopped scratching her favourite itch long enough she would find out why. Some Western critic I was reading, I forget his name, was sneering at the kind of things his teachers used to talk about, the imagination for instance. He says the word was frequently used but he never found out what it meant. Depressing, isn't it?

Some years ago I was amazed when I finally got around to reading Macaulay's famous statement about one shelf of books in a Western library is worth and etc. He was wrong, of course, but the context modifies it. He says if England had closed its doors during the Renaissance it would have been a very much poorer place. I felt this made him sound less jingoistic, and anyway they should read the way he writes about Puritans.

Bye for now. I think I shall treat myself to a mopey evening.

Love

Dear David,

Read a weird article today, or at least an article about weird goings-on. It was commenting on some Asians in Britain who (in quotes) would rather give up a job than shake hands with male associates. And these are men, not women. 'Many educated people are devoting themselves to religion and living on social security,' one of the people interviewed said. I wondered how come they didn't mind the cheques handed out by the Brits whose hands they won't otherwise touch. They even send second-generation girls back to some dump in Pakistan to marry local yokels. Apparently the Brits didn't mix here either during colonial times, but why go back to backward ideas? Depressing, isn't it? I sometimes wonder why I watch or read the news. Round and round. Poor old Queen's Diamonds almost sounds like sanity by comparison. What to do. Make myself a mug of tea I think.

Love

The bai is intrigued by the number of images of Hindu gods Rina has in her living room. Why do you have Hindu gods in your home she says, and no Christian ones?

Show ke liye, she says, using the mish-mash phrase used in these parts to indicate an arty display. It is curious, she thinks, how many gods she had ended up visiting. Sri Nathji in Nathadwar is one of her favourites, a dark god, with slanting, glittering, diamond eyes. She liked his style: new clothes for every darshan, a rose in an upturned palm. She had watched the women crowding in as soon as the temple doors were opened, calling out his name, staggering out in a swoon.

The streets leading to his shrine were full of shops which had pictures of him in all kinds of outfits: yellow silk in one, shocking pink in another. Some were hand-painted, others were printed postcards or shiny prints in tacky tin frames. She had bought as many as she could.

At the government guest house where she stayed, peacocks roamed the rooms, and sun birds hovered over the hibiscus flowers. She sat at a table on the lawn, listening to the peacocks' harsh cries.

It was Father de Leury, a French priest who taught at her mother's school in Poona, who had introduced her and others who were interested to the Hindu world amidst which they lived. Father de Leury was considered a bit mad, because he had given up wearing a cassock, and wore kurta pyjamas and lived in the city amongst the Brahmins.

Madness was fairly common. To dance to Elvis Presley's music (music?) was mad. Old Mr Crasta had demonstrated a few steps to show just how mad and bad this was. Miss L who fancied Father B who turned red in her presence was mad. Mr F who painted Our Lady in a sari was mad. What would he do next, put Christ in a dhoti?

Father de Leury talked about Tukaram, and read out some of his poems. Tukaram argues with God, attacks the Brahmin establishment, and has his manuscripts thrown into the river for his pains. Of course his family starves. He ends every poem with 'says Tuka'. She liked that. Says Tuka. He is colloquial, down-to-earth, irresistible. The voice set something in her free.

Father de Leury had been to Pandharpur, walking with the pilgrims, singing Tukaram's songs. Many years later she too travelled to Pandharpur (by train, alas, not on foot), and to Dehu and Alandi, all the places associated with the saint-poet, and she offered a coconut to Vithoba and his wife Rakhumai, for a friend about to do an exam. (He passed.) She was glad the barren Poona hills which Tukaram called home are her hills too. The Himalayas are more spectacular, but picture-postcardish. These hills are more real, always brown, and black with rock, except when they are grey-blue in the distance or in the sudden dusk.

She knew that she would go away, but always come back, to see if the hills were still where she had left them.

It's a foldable plywood cupboard, and one of the hinges is broken, so the door is slightly askew. Near the cupboard, in a corner, is the camp cot her father took with him when he was posted in those outlandish places, till he died in 1943. Inside the cupboard are his suits and ties, a solar topee, some books on law and revenue, and a scrapbook in which he had pasted news items that interested him, written out sketches for stories, and poems he was working on, scratching out a word here, a phrase there. What was it like, she wonders, to be trying to write in the tribal districts of the Central Provinces, haunted by the sound of a distant train.

A few loose sheets contain a complete story about the tribals among whom he lived and worked. It is called True Tales the Tiger Did Not Tell. 'His people lived in the Supkhar Range of the Central Provinces. Land where the hoot of an owl harried their slumbers and filled their waking dreams with evil to come. Tigers they could see or climb the nearest tree, but what could one do against evil spirits that hooted and hunted at night? So this son of the loins of a hundred Gonds was christened Ghurwa (rubbish heap) and was called Baiga, so that any unhallowed spirit, prowling in the night, might be confused...'

She recognizes the typewriter on which the story is typed. It is the heavy old Remington portable kept in her grandfather's room.

He also writes notes to himself in the book. 'The Struggle for Mexican Independence was condemned by the Pope. Is this true? Find out. 29/9/36 Raipur.' 'I was presented today with a book. *The Pathetic Fallacy* by Llewelyn Powys. Ballu (B.R. Chaobal) gave it to me as a mark of friendship. The book is a blind argument against Christianity. I am not afraid to read it.'

She had brought her father's notebook with her to Bombay. It was her only real contact with him. She was amazed, the first time she saw it, to discover that she and her father had something in common. She kept notebooks too in school and wrote down all the phrases she liked and hoped to introduce into her English compositions. She has seven pages of phrases from George Eliot and Jane Austen. 'A man of sterling insignificance.' She liked that. In the summer when there were no compositions to write, she practised on her friends who were away. Dear Rita, she would write, There is a Chinese proverb, which says that there is a time to fish, and a time for the drying of nets; Dear Pat, Yesterday I met a man of sterling insignificance.

Then there were the notebooks the nuns asked them to keep. The Book of Acts. Make an act, dear, the nuns would say. Today for the love of Jesus I will not eat any sweets. Today for love of Mary I did not tell a lie even though I wanted to.

In spite of her inventiveness, she was not chosen to be one of the confirmed members of Our Lady's Sodality. Her desk was not tidy. Her tennis shoes used to stink. She was caught playing leapfrog during the break. She did not care about the Sodality but she did not want to be left out. We will wait a year, said Sister Thomas, it will be good for your character.

A retreat was also good for the character. For three days the girls had to be silent and prayerful. They had to meditate on their sins. They had to pray to know if they had a vocation.

The girls who lived far away in Range Hills or Salisbury Park stayed in the hostel for those three days. They were happy to do so. They hoped to catch a glimpse of Sister Margaret without her cap on. The boarders had seen her and said her hair was brown and cut very short.

The priest would tell them a lot about the Devil during the retreat. The Devil is a busy fellow, seeking whom he may devour. She used to wonder if the Devil would devour the Anglo-Indians who jived at parties. She would have liked to know how to jive, to fling herself about with such abandon. She used to wonder if the Devil knew that Betty vamped on the piano when Miss Copland said Excuse me girls I shall be back in a minute.

She laughs when she thinks about all this and wonders if school is still like that. But it wasn't funny at the time. The Redemptorist priests called in for retreats were specialists in fire and brimstone. They did their job well. Even now, damnation is never really far from her mind.

The electrician, Rina decides, is the man in her life. There is no one he doesn't know, plumbers, TV repairers, painters. I have known him all my life, he says about anyone he sends along. You can trust him absolutely. And it's true. You can leave him the flat, or them in the flat, and disappear. Nothing else will.

Golconda, he says, looking at an old print on her wall. You've been there?

I've lived in Hyderabad, he says, had a job there. And another one in Nairobi, till the project was over. He is full of surprises.

Don't let the parrots out, he says, as he fixes the wires of the hanging lamp for the twentieth time. They'll short-circuit the flat. She is embarrassed when she has to call him the twenty-first time. I keep an eye on them, she says, but they're so quick.

He has a small shop, six by six, with a room above it. But he has a plot of land in Uran, he says, and is building a house there. When he is away, his wife sits in the shop, in a pretty sari and a fair amount of gold jewellery. Or his sons, who speak English to her when she speaks Hindi to them. They have been to college. They have learnt their father's work, but are looking for other jobs. They smile and say good-morning when she walks by.

She lies awake listening to the cock crow, and the crows caw, and the clink of bottles as the milkman arrives. It's a good life, she thinks, all things considered.

Eunice de Souza

Dear David,

The male parrot is very frus these days. He wants to mate with the female but doesn't seem to know how. There are always the courting preliminaries and then nothing happens. I don't know if it is because he was trapped as a baby and is living in a human home. He's developed these heart-rending cries. I'm going to ask someone at the Natural History Society if they can tell me how to let him go, preferably in some woody place outside Bombay where there aren't too many crows. I'm worried about whether he'll be able to look for food for himself.

By the way, at least one neighbour thinks I am a bit mad. The other day I was walking around the flat doing odd jobs and the older parrot was sitting on my head, literally, as he often does. When the doorbell rang, I forgot he was there and opened the door. Poor Mrs A was most startled to see the parrot perched like that and let out a little scream.

Will you be back this summer for a bit?

Love, Love

As she leaves home in the morning, she scribbles the word Pass on her packet of cigarettes to remind her to renew her quarterly pass to Churchgate.

At the counter, the clerk looks at her card, looks at her, smiles, calls another clerk, mumbles to him, and then they both snicker.

Is there something wrong with my ID card? she asks irritably.

Madam, one of them says, photo is old. You are not looking like this now.

What difference does it make? she asks with even more irritation.

Before they can reply, the man behind her in the queue pipes in, If accident is happening, how they will identify corpse?

Oh!

This time I am giving, the clerk says, but next time I am not giving.

Okay, she says, I'll change the photograph.

Accident is definitely happening, she thinks. For reasons that escape her and everyone else, there are people who think it amusing to throw stones at the trains. In the last few months several commuters have lost an eye, and at least one was killed by the force of the stone. And since the day bombs exploded all over Bombay, commuters are alarmed by unexpected noises or the first sign of smoke. Seeing a flame, some women had once jumped out of the train, only to be killed by a train racing down the parallel track. The railways had said there was no flame. There were angry exchanges in the newspapers. These women were educated, one enraged citizen said, they would not have jumped without good reason.

All announcements are made in three languages. Do not endanger your life by crossing the tracks. Please use the foot overbridge. As she moves back because the train is coming in, she catches sight of two small boys gazing at the violently coloured cakes in the railway tea stall.

A set piece, she thinks, but the longing is real, so is the stoicism. They do not wheedle or whine or pluck at anyone's clothes. They begin to drift away.

She goes up to them and says, Would you like something to eat?

The older one nods briefly.

Choose, she says.

The small boy asks his even smaller brother to choose for both of them. The stall attendant gives them two pink cakes wrapped in newspaper and two glasses of tea. They sit down on the platform floor and unwrap the package.

Will they be there next day at the same time on the off chance that she is there? She hopes so. They are not.

No one says it any longer, even as a joke: When the Revolution comes!

When all else fails, try a pedicure. She takes off her chappals. Warm, scented water is pure bliss.

Magazines?

Yes. She does not want idle chatter to disturb the moment.

Shampoo?

Yes.

Blow Dry?

Yes

Bliss.

Fin de siecle? Maybe. Except that it's more like siecles, and not just at the fin. A bright pink pastry to counter human history? One fledgling parrot rescued from the crows? Of course there are five million organizations doing five million things. Of course Chicken Soup is full of stories about human good. Of course there's Tukaram and Greene. Of course she loves a good meal, a pedicure, and gossip with friends. So then?

Mad or what?

There, thank goodness, someone's finally said it. For some time she's thought if she hears that word tolerant again she'll scream. Soft on Hindutva. Praful Bidwai: 'Hinduism may be pluralistic, but is it really all that tolerant? The claim is unconvincing for a religion that in reality is inseparable from casteism and hierarchical social order. So long as people are lynched for defying religious prohibitions on caste inter-marriage, and the Dalits are oppressed and women subordinated in religion's name, the claim to tolerance will fail.' Feb 6, 1999.

PLAFF, as her friend Vera would say at moments of high drama.

Dear David,

Had a call from Sonalini yesterday. She's worked in some of these areas where scary things are happening, the Dang area and Orissa. She says in some of these hamlets people don't know what a government babu looks like. One woman she met had only one sari, and would wash one end of it and hold it out to dry while covering herself with the other end. They were on a leprosy project there, run by Christian missionaries. She says a friend of

hers signed a protest letter against the harassm
of missionaries and the next day had a phone call
from a goon. The worrying thing is that it is not the
sixty plus but fairly young men in their teens or early
twenties who are really violent. I told her she must
write about it, so few people know these areas. She
says that if there was a dispensary at all it was run by
missionaries. It's all getting out of hand and everyone
is appalled.

Saw a bizarre item in the papers today. Apparently,
the getaway car used by Godse after the murder of
Gandhi is still around in Bareilly. It was sold by a
broker to some guy who later sold it to another. It's
been entered in several vintage car rallies. A mob
once threatened to burn it.

Write soon, Love

Vera is staying over. They will have pizza and wine
(no cooking) and in the morning treat themselves
to breakfast at the restaurant near the race course.
She likes going there, especially during the racing
season, with the syces exercising the horses, and
jockeys practising on the tracks.

She is interested in lives that otherwise do not
touch hers. The trim and tiny jockeys, the owners

covered in soft and shapeless fat. Not creamy, like successful corporate types, or sleek, like well-groomed pussycats.

The mint tea was pleasant, but there's a mistake in the bill, an extra tea and coffee they did not have. They send the bill back, and watch the horses till the waiter returns.

When she watches the news, she looks for the people in the background. The woman entering a shop, a young couple holding hands. She likes to know what people are doing when they are not bobbing endlessly in front of the wall, or dying of hunger, or just dying, as they seem to do so insistently and predictably. It seems important that the woman keeps entering that shop; that the vegetable man put up a new board saying LEAKS PARCELY AVACADO when a politician is shown kicking a picture of Rushdie in the face while his followers laugh and applaud.

She thinks of all those endless debates about the ordinary man as tragic hero and thinks really he doesn't have to be a hero at all, tragic or otherwise. He must just put up a new board for vegetables, or she must cook an excellent sweet daal, and he and she light up a corner of the world, and are not ordinary any more, if they ever were.

Well, ordinary people and silly asses. This is silly ass time, slack time before the term ends, and management experts will be called in for faculty improvement. She has been to one such and refuses to go again. She remembers the fellow. He slowly drew a horizontal across the board, then turned it into an arrow, and then slowly wrote GOAL. We must all have goals. An idiot female talks about values. If your house is burning, would you rush in and save your money or your Bible? If you save your Bible, you are spiritual. If you save your money you are material. One of the cynics says, but if you save your money you can buy another Bible.

Standing at the bus stop she watches the man with the wheelbarrow. He is piling the rubbish he has swept off the streets into it—dry leaves, plastic, bits of paper. He overloads the card. As he walks, bits of paper and leaves fall off and back on to the road. He walks on regardless. She wonders which myth can be found to glorify this futile exercise.

Dear David,

You have a new girlfriend and she looks like Winona Ryder and she doesn't want me to visit you in the summer? What have you been telling her? I suppose I shall have to write less often so that she doesn't get hyper. If she looks like Winona Ryder why is she insecure? Anyway, no bad-mouthing, I shall become interested in good deeds. Your mum was saying the other day that she and I should both go to visit you! Eeks is right.

Do you remember the woman upstairs who was always screaming at her little daughter? She turned up the other day with a box of almonds, walnuts, apricots, pitachios. Nestled in the middle was a copy of *The God of Small Things*! Now that is really fame. She asked if I knew she got three crores for the book. Poor Arundhati is never going to live down that three crores. Every article on her mentions it first thing. Anyway the neighbour says she is 'thinking of writing a novel and making a lot of money.' In Gujarati? says I. You know Arundhati? Ask her for publisher, says she. I don't know Arundhati. I am showing you when I write. Ouch.

And ouch again, beautiful. Missing you.

Love, Love

Swine, Rina thinks as she listens to David on the phone saying he was feeling stale and needed to re-energize himself. Also he was feeling randy. Rina said she was too though no doubt she should be thinking of higher things at her age. Anyway, says dear David, keep clear of Jay. He's nothing but trouble.

She should have known. Years ago he was in the audience at a talk she had given somewhere, and she had quoted Thoreau: 'The majority of men live lives of quiet desperation', and David (that is who he turned out to be), sat up, and she had thought Aha a broody type *and* with high cheekbones.

They had gone off to a nearby café and talked and talked over two cups of tea till the proprietor had waddled out from behind his counter and said, Giving tuition or what?

Utter is sitting on her step shelling green peas.

That kept upstairs. She is getting married.

Oh! To her boss?

No, someone else. But the boss will remain her business partner.

Mr Chopra will be happy that his neighbour is becoming respectable, she says.

Chopraji does a lot of bur-bur, Utter says. He is a

fool. Lots of furniture going upstairs, she adds. One sofa set, red velvet. Very nice. Looks like foreign.

Oh!

Utter's mother-in-law comes out smoking a bidi. Your bai told me the puppy you were looking after died, she says.

Yes.

It's very painful, isn't it, the mother-in-law says. I've looked after dogs and parrots too, but I couldn't bear it when they were old.

Yes.

She is touched that Utter's mother-in-law has talked to her like this. It's the first real connection she has made in Queen's Diamonds.

Outside the bai and the electrician who solves all her problems, she thinks. She is so used to them that she would find it difficult ever to leave Queen's Diamonds, even though it isn't the most thrilling place to live in.

Stone Age men lived in Delhi, she reads. They still do, she thinks sourly. Teachers' wages have gone up courtesy the Central Government, but so has the workload. One has to go in to sign the muster whether one has invigilation that day or not, spend a minimum of four to five hours in college six days a week whether one's classes are over or not, mark exam papers in college. The vacations have been cut, so has the number of days of casual leave.

It's a strange mentality, she thinks, punitive in a pointless way. What on earth would they sit around doing on the days when there were no lectures and no exams and the students were at home preparing for their finals? Maybe she should retire early. It would be a relief not to hear that alarm clock early in the morning, and to be able to lounge around doing nothing in particular, reading, writing, going to handloom sales, having lunch with a friend. Maybe she would dye her hair blue and totter around the world. Or catch up with the relatives she hadn't seen for donkey's years. Her father's youngest brother was still in Nagpur. He was said to be one of the nicest of the lot, and like her father in many ways. She had hardly seen him as a child. He was always away in the force in some remote place or the other. She'd catch up with him at least. The others had all gone away, to Canada, Australia, England, France. There was the occasional Christmas card, no more, and then she would write back, late as usual. Age, was it, or seasonal melancholy? She'd never given much thought to family before.

Roots, she detests the word, it has been used and abused so much. She decides to annoy herself further by thinking of the ways in which her family annoys her: the aunts who think that because she is single her time is at their disposal, the endless conversation about illnesses and problems. She decides to ring Vera and complain.

When she finally gets through, Vera says, Jay was over last evening. He thinks he is your blue-eyed boy.

This is weird. I haven't seen him for months. We talk on the phone. Where does the blue-eyed stuff come in?

Oh! says Vera, I told him you handle him with kid gloves.

But where does handling him with kid gloves or any other kind of gloves come in?

We didn't spend the whole evening talking about you.

I know you didn't. I just asked what the context of the remarks was.

Listen, I've got to go, Vera says.

Half an hour later the phone rings. I'm sorry, Vera says, I was just blowing my top.

What happened?

It's my bloody father-in-law. He expects Mulk and me to spend time with him as soon as we come home because he isn't well. Silly bastard. He even asked me why I didn't touch his feet when he came back from hospital.

Mm...

I feel like strangling him. I suppose all these bullies get sentimental in their old age.

Mm...

Anyway, I'm coming over tomorrow. We can go out for lunch or something. I'll pick up some beer on the way.

Fine, just don't complain about the cigarette smoke.

Oh God! Okay.

One way of getting rid of aggro, Rina has discovered, is to take part in panel discussions on subjects she is irritated by. One can say with all due respect and then say a whole lot of nasty things. So she is pleased when an invitation on Indian writing in English arrives. It will be the same old crap, how writing in English exists at the expense of writing in the other languages and so on. That three crores again. Of course they don't mean just money but all the hidden treasures which are unknown because the writers in English get all the attention.

So Rina says (and they no doubt will say she is just

aping Rushdie) it is lucky the writers in other languages are less known because then one can make all sorts of claims for them. If they are translated and they are less than absolutely thrilling one can say they are lost in translation. And if one says well the good work comes through in translation one can say there are no universal standards and anyway it is all a plot by dead white males and some living ones too.

Rina feels much better. She decides to go for a haircut and shampoo. She will try a new hairstyle. So there. She decides to write to David whether Winona Ryder likes it or not.

It is after the death of a stray pup that she has her first real conversation with Jay, really the first in all those years. She had picked up this mangy, malnourished pup near the temple at the end of the road and taken it to an animal clinic. Perhaps it would have died anyway but she was devastated when she saw it after three weeks in the clinic, covered with ticks, without a rag to lie on. She took it home again and on the advice of friends who had dogs fed it with a syringe. The first day home it climbed onto her lap. The second day it walked around the flat and sniffed at everything. The third day it died.

She rings Jay and says talk to me, say anything, and he does. He says it feels like this when we have invested so much in a person or thing, and he doesn't mean money, he isn't feeling too good himself. We can't go round saying maya maya all is maya because that's not how we are, he says. Sometimes, he says, he sees a funeral procession on the road and he wonders what the man's life was all about, or the woman's, and then he suddenly hears the car behind him honking to tell him to get a move on.

She says she must let the parrots go one of these days, she worries about what would happen to them if anything happened to her. He says there are a lot of fruit trees near his farmhouse and not so many crows and maybe they would make it.

She thinks dear God I don't want to be involved in life at all. The few feathers strewn in her flowerpot is all that's left of the baby pigeon that had looked at her with a bright and beady eye. The little pup trembling with weakness. Millions streaming out of Kosovo. But what is the alternative—to be a spirit hovering on the dark side of the room? Anguish, the word is anguish, and she doesn't want it. She is distressed to find herself so distressed. That's not what she wants at all.

Should she write to the clinic? They will say it's only a woman upset about her dog and there are so many women here upset about their dogs, that is if they bother to say anything at all. One of the women who had also brought a stray to the clinic looked at the pup and said he's in such bad shape you must put him to sleep but she could not after he had wagged his tail at her.

It is Easter Sunday. She reads the Pope's speech though she normally does not have much time for the Pope. He speaks of the need to have the 'audacity to hope'. The phrase brings tears to her eyes.

Well, if she's looking for a sign perhaps Mrs Castellino is as good as any. She met her at the clinic where she had brought her old dog, who could not even stand any more. Mrs Castellino promised to look after the stray pup during the three days Rina would be away for a seminar. She kept her word. Though her own old dog died on a Tuesday, Mrs Castellino went on Wednesday and Thursday to see the pup, and it was a very long distance, which she travelled by bus.

She rings Mrs Castellino when she gets back from the seminar, and Mrs Castellino says, Bring the pup home. If he's going to die let him at least die on your lap, not of neglect in the clinic. I'll come and show you how to look after him. Again she travels a long distance to her home, on Good Friday night, and Holy Saturday morning, and teaches her how to mix the Farex, how to administer it with a syringe. She says call me any time you want. And Mrs Castellino is a lady she had met for the first time at the clinic.

Mrs Castellino is not a social worker. She just likes animals and birds, Munna, she says to the pup as she puts him on her lap, Munna, you're a beautiful pup.

Perhaps the great revelation never does come. Maybe there are just changes in the list of people one wants to machine gun every day. The neighbour downstairs who plays the same monotonous bhajan as loud as she can every morning at 6.45 and who says my neighbours are Hindu, there is demand. And Lily Languish who is chortling in the staffroom and saying simperingly I love to sing, once I start I just can't stop, and she proceeds to sing in the bloody staffroom. And Smarm who says what are you going to share with us today? Share? Tell us about. Why can't he just say tell us about, where does bloody sharing come into it?

She tries to ring Vera who has not come to college that day. There is something wrong with the line. She rings 199. A bright recorded female voice says that this is the local assistance service of Mahanagar Telephone Nigam, and she should dial the required number without disconnecting after she hears the beep. She begins to dial the number. After the first digit the bright voice says this facility is not available on this service. Hell, she thinks and tries again. The same thing happens. How, she wonders, do we keep sane in this country?

A novelist friend rings and says for God's sake don't go into a decline I won't forgive you if you do, someone has to talk sense at those syllabus meetings. And she says, You should have been at the last one. One guy said there are no poets after T.S. Eliot, and he didn't want Arundhati Roy on the syllabus because, he said, only Time Can Tell, We Are Too Near, and I said yes, maybe time can tell but we can also tell, we can't leave her out and that is final.

According to the glossies people are already planning millennium parties. She knows what she will do, she will sleep through the whole thing and forget to write the correct year on her cheques.

What's with this millennium frenzy, nothing is going to change. She will stand. She will stand at the bus stop at the gate, the bus driver will wear his look of heavy irony, the trains will be hot and crowded, Lily Languish will arrive late in college, eat a dosa, have a nap and disappear, and nobody will be able to throw her out, it's not for lack of trying, she has contacts.

Look, she says to the bai, they are writing about your dangerlok in the papers.

The bai is interested so she translates bits of the articles she has been reading.

They even quote you, she says to the bai. You remember what you are always saying? Hota hai; it happens. The mish-mash language she speaks with the bai isn't up to translating what follows. The writer says, 'I was struck by the amazing brevity with which those two words encapsulated an entire approach to life. In a flash they make every deprivation an ephemeral aspect of an unreal drama in which pleasure and pain are a passing phenomenon. Hota hai means that for every bad power-cut there was possibly a worse one before and there could be a worse one in future.'

How do they know what I say? The bai asks.

Lots of people feel the way you do, she says.

Utter does not feel that way. The secretary has put up a fresh list of people who have not paid their dues, and Utter's name is at the top again. She summons the watchman, gives him a cup of tea, and then makes him unlock the notice board. She tears off the list. I own three flats, she says, who is he to tell me to pay my dues.

Watch out, there may be a stray bullet whizzing by: TOI Feb 6, '99... This is in sharp contrast to the situation not very long ago when the underworld boasted that gang wars did not affect the common man. But the police now say that the mafia has changed its tactics. 'The triggerman used in the contract killing is no longer a ganster or a professional criminal,' revealed a senior police officer. 'These jobless youngsters are so ignorant about firearms that someone has to cock the pistol for them before they are sent on a hit job.' The new hitmen tend to choose public places for their killings as it is easy for them to escape in the chaos created by firing. Police attribute the high number of casualties to the edgy nerves of the first-time killers.

Dangerlok

The bai says there's a Meena Kumari film would she turn the TV on. The film seems to be over, but there's another one on with that blank-faced pretty boy Mithun as hero. She watches with some interest because one of the villains turns out to be a Goan, D'souza. The hero hits D'souza so long and so hard that the fellow should be dead by now. Then the police arrive.

Now, see what happens, says the bai.
Have you seen the film before? she asks.
No.
So how do you know?
It always happens, she says, and laughs her merry laugh. A crowd of schoolboys rushes into the police station. They fold their hands and pray to the police officer. Please release our Shankar, says one boy, bursting into tears. The police officer does so. The heroine who is lurking in the background has brought the children here. The hero has been neglecting her, and she has had to dance for his attention, alternately sticking out her cast-iron breasts or her butt to a merry tune. In her merry way she had once locked his door and slipped the key down her cleavage. It is a lock that anyone with a hairpin could pick in a second. But he doesn't, otherwise how will he get into her cleavage. Not that that's his intention of course. He just wants to unlock

the door, get inside, and have a cup of tea.
Bingo. Happy Ending.

A neighbour tells her their names are being taken off the list of the ration shop next door, and they must now go to one not far from the buffalo sheds. She will have to go personally and sign for this form, no one else can do it for her.

The new ration shop is behind the public loo, the new public loo, and the only pucca building in that area. There is already a long queue of people waiting to hand in or collect forms. There is no sign of the ration shop man, and it is already an hour after opening time. It's Sunday, someone says, he'll come when he feels like it.

Finally the man waddles in. Everyone is riveted by him.

Now he is opening the shop.

Now his man is sweeping the floor.

Now he is doing his puja.

He has to, says a wag, otherwise how will he make his money.

Oh no! He is leaving the shop!

No, he's just going to wash his face.

He is opening the books.

He is fiddling with his mobile, which isn't working.

Tell him not to fiddle with the phone. We've been waiting two hours.

He is accepting the first form.

Oh good! Someone has forgotten to xerox the old ration card.

One less person in the queue.

By comparison, the bus driver is a saint. When he rounds the corner of the road and finds rickshaws double parked on both sides, he folds his arms over the wheel, and hunches over it without a word.

Either that or a coronary, she thinks, or both.

The rickshaw-walas emerge from tea shops or huddles with pals, grinning foolishly.

The driver straightens up and sounds the horn.

Double line down the middle, shouts the ticket collector to all those who have scrambled on.

Double line down the middle.

The corner at the other end of the lane is usually peaceful. Women gather round the well, drawing water and washing clothes on the road. There is a tea-stall under the bougainvillea, with a large kettle always on the boil. There is an autorickshaw and taxi stand there, and the taxi drivers play cards on the bonnet of one of the taxis, or read a newspaper. They are always glad to see her. It means a whopping fare. She indulges herself in a taxi ride to college once in a while, for no special reason. Justa. Simbly.

If she leaves early enough, there isn't too much traffic. But the whole point of a taxi is not to leave early enough. So there is traffic, more on some days than others. What's the matter, she asks. Why is there so much traffic? Why aren't we moving?

There's a jam, he says.

She knows there is a traffic jam, she wants to know why.

He shrugs his shoulders. It's Tuesday, he says.

Tomorrow he will shrug his shoulders and say it's Wednesday. He is not of an inquiring turn of mind.

The wedding invitation from a neighbour reads, 'This is only a tiny message but it's written just for you to find time in your busy life to give us a moment or two as Baldwin walks up the aisle with Hyacinth on April 20 at which time we'd love to have you witness the two of us in matrimonial oneness while we say "I Do" at St. What not's Church and at 7.30 pm sharp at St. Theresa's Hall we shall rendezvous.'

The message weaves its way along the edges of an

eight-inch cutout of a girl in a bonnet and a fellow in a morning suit standing with their foreheads touching.

She decides to take it to Poona to show her mother who is amused by these things. Her mother can't stand the MCs (masters of ceremonies) who never stop talking during the reception and feel they must be witty and bawdy. Her mother quotes a recent witticism she heard at a wedding reception. The groom was a Maths teacher. In the classroom, the MC said, the teacher had to deal with figures and curves. And now he would *really* have to deal with figures and curves.

The Bishop who performed the ceremony assured the couple that 'life was like a sweet and sour sauce'.

Mr Lobo died last week, her mother says.

Oh!

Mr Lobo used to sing the Dies Irae alone at the Mass for the Dead. Note by unhurried note he built a world, contained, sombre, magnificent. It was completely outside her, impersonal, yet it took her, Mr Lobo and everyone she knew and didn't know, to a place where they need not weep or plead and beat their breasts in an endless mea culpa.

She used to think that she would not mind dying if Mr Lobo would sing the Dies Irae while she lay there, like a fish on a slab that's been there a day too long. But Mr Lobo is dead, and with him the ancient chants of the monks, rising in the dark cold dawns.

It is not the passing of the Latin prayers she minds. There was always the English in the right-hand column of the prayer book. It's not the English or the Tamil or the Konkani. It's the strumming and yodelling to sweet Jesus that sets her teeth on edge.

She watches her mother make the age-old gesture, come up the stairs, take off her rimless glasses, put them on the piano and then go in to tea. Her grandmother used to brew the tea in a white pot with pink flowers on it, and cover it with a cosy to keep it warm in case she was a little late coming back from the boys' school where she taught.

Sometimes teachers from her mother's school used to drop in to chat. This always annoyed her grandfather, especially if it was Miss Myrtle, because they would chat for a very long time, and then go down the stairs and chat some more on the pavement. What can they have to talk about, her grandfather raged.

They have just spent the whole day in school together.

So what, she thought, but of course could not say so what to her grandfather, he would have had a stroke.

Go downstairs and tell your mother I want some tea.

She dawdled on each step, counting ten before she moved to the next. She did not particularly want to meet Miss Myrtle who would say, And what class are you in, dear? Miss Myrtle had asked her that a hundred times.

Ah, here is the little lovely, says Miss Myrtle, it must be time for tea.

Miss Myrtle would then prattle for another ten minutes at least.

Soon a voice would thunder from the balcony. Miss Myrtle would look up, beaming. Ah! There you are, she would shrill to the grandfather, lovely day, isn't it. Toodle-oo.

She used to sleep on the same bed as her mother, and sometimes put her foot on her mother's feet and her arm around her. She could not imagine ever sleeping in any other way. She has one thing in common with her mother after all these years, Rina thinks. She likes men with high cheekbones like her father's.

Rina's mother had never wanted her to leave Poona

and had urged her to find a lecturer's job in the city. And she had tried. She remembers her first interview very well. Five men were sitting behind the desk, but it was only the one with eyes the colour of stone who asked the questions.

Why did you go to Bombay to study? Aren't there colleges in Poona?

Yes, but my mother wanted me to go to a college for women. We have a cousin who is a nun there, and my mother thought she would look after me.

And when you went abroad, did you go to a college for women?

Yes.

Was there anyone there to look after you?

No.

So how did they send you abroad if they are so particular? He looks at the others to see if they appreciate his style.

Do you know any language?

Yes, Konkani.

Konkani is not a language. It's a dialect.

Her hands are clammy but she says, I think there is another view of the subject.

She had begun to loathe a species she had not yet recognized as a species, and for which she had not yet found a name.

She wakes up one morning to find The Muse typing out a message on her Olivetti. The Muse? The last time she thought The Muse had turned up a poet-friend had assured her that she should concentrate on her teaching. She had thrown the poems out along with all the juvenalia junk she had brought along quite sentimentally from Poona; newspapers she had written, complete with ads for Aunty Margaret's Tea shoppe, and crudely drawn cartoons; a story after an overdose of Dickens, about Mrs Langley who lived in a slum in England and had died slowly and painfully. Her three children had stormed Heaven to recover her, but they had died too, slowly and painfully.

Thus engrossed in the travails of the world, she had written a poem for her English teacher wishing her well as she passed through this vale of sorrows. It was her first poem and she had shown it to her mother. Her mother had said that as far as she knew the English teacher was perfectly happy, so she had kept the poem for another occasion.

Now she wanted something multi-layered but not amorphous, something that could include children burning in a jeep, bright green parrots screeching across the sky, party animals and Utter dressing her gods.

All right, she thinks, she'll give The Muse another chance.

Pahari Parrots

I

Not for'him the cold swathes
of pine and mist,
hook-nosed king of a succulent sky.

In his wire-mesh cage
He gives nothing away.

I buy him on impulse.
He makes my flat his home:
Rubber plants, candles, pencils, plastic
make a fine confetti...

Princely wastrel of a
lost kingdom.

II

She peers through lattice windows
at the empty street
the long afternoon broken
only by the squawks of parrots.
The air is humid
but there is no rain.

Dangerlok

III

Sometimes we compare notes:
I talk about the parrots
She talks about her children.
She tells me little K cries for effect.
If I get home after dark, I tell her,
They look at me with sad, reproachful eyes.

At dusk, all three of us and
all three of them
are melancholic.
Both want to sit on her lap.
Both want to sit on my left shoulder.
I smoke and down a vodka.

Soon I'll be a whiskery old lady
mumbling in my gums
hobbling about
two parrots in my hair.

IV

At the sight of campari the parrots make
little weak-kneed noises.
Toth pulls the glass one way
Tothi the other

both hang on when I pull.
It's a regular bar-room brawl.

V

Spring, and the trees are translucent.
One can hardly tell
leaf from parrot
berries from beak
red splash on wing
from veins that tingle.

VI

Two trees and a garbage heap.
The garbage brings the barbets.
The parrots love the peepul tree.
There's a bulbul singing in the ashoka.
Throw in sparrows, crows and mynahs
you have your common city garden
complete with pandemonium at dawn.

The lady on the third floor says
We should cut down the trees
she can't sleep for the noise.

Lady, you're a fingernail
scratching a blackboard.

She is quite pleased with her efforts and decides to send copies to Megan and David to ask their opinion. But she will have to look for a Post Office in town. She can't deal with the gnome again.

She finds one that seems to have been refurbished. There are plastic flowers on the tables, and computers at many of the counters. Above each counter there is a sign that says Multipurpose Counter. It should sell stamps.

It should, but it doesn't, the clerk says, even more amiably, and then goes back to gazing vaguely at the ceiling.

She reads an extraordinary report in the papers entitled 'Myths about Manners'. Apparently, those who are unfailingly courteous are inclined to be depressed and sad, while it is the cheery and well-adjusted folk who are inclined to be rude.

Well, she thinks, I prefer them depressed and sad. She mentions the report to a colleague in her department who has been complaining about students being a lot less well mannered than they used to be a few years ago. Students today don't stand aside for a teacher at the coffee-machine, or wait at the top of the stairs when they see a teacher walking up.

She could add to that list, certainly. Students seated in trains and buses would not offer her a seat if she was standing. Not that she would have accepted, but even so, just the offer would have been pleasant.

It's odd, her colleague says, and I can't account for it. It's not just the nouveaux riche, it seems to be everybody.

I wonder if it is like that in other colleges, she says, or just ours.

There's not much they can do about it anyway. Talking about manners in class would be too schoolmarmy. Slip it in, maybe, during a lecture on Jane Austen's ideas about manners and see what they say. She had tried once, saying something about saying thank you to those who work for us, liftmen and the like. The class had thought it very amusing.

David writes to her about the poems, and also sends a *Guide to a Well-Behaved Parrot*. There's a chapter on Games Parrots Play. One game is called I'll drop it, and you pick it up. It's a game initiated by the parrot who keeps dropping his toys and expecting you to pick them up. She knows that one. That's one of the ways she keeps fit. 'I believe,' the book says, 'any human who will spend a few moments picking up a repeatedly dropped trinket for a bird is well on the way to being a trusted, treasured friend for life.'

Stimulating the Reluctant Talker is a lot less helpful. Watch lots of Tarzan movies, the author says, yell at television sports activities, in bird screams if possible. Sing to the bird when you run the shower, dishwasher or vacuum cleaner.

No, she thinks, not Tarzan movies. The parrots will just have to put up with news on the BBC.

Dear David,

You're keeping all my letters in case you decide to write a biography of me when I'm ever so famous? What an appalling idea! Whatever you do don't tell the truth!

I've just been reading an awful biography of Nissim Ezekiel. The biographer says Nissim's family refused to talk to him, so did the women N was allegedly involved with, and in any case the biographer lost interest halfway through because N is heterosexual and he is a gay activist who would rather write about a gay writer! Isn't it weird? My letter seems full of exclamation marks today and there are more. He even refers to one of his sources who wants to remain unnamed as 'Mr X'! Eeks. I know you'll never refer to Mr X, especially because none of my exes want to be referred to at all. Jay is pretty paranoid now that I have started writing. I've told him I have no interest in what Vera calls 'vaginal monologues'.

One of the parrots put on a huge display when Jay dropped in the other day after ages. The parrot sat on my shoulder and kept nibbling my cheek to show who belonged to whom. Jay was amazed. The parrot has never done that before or since.

No Dibs, I love you dearly but I will not write down what I remember of my life. I'd rather forget it! It's a bit like that bus of ours which goes round and round. I remember a line from a poem: 'I head for the abyss with monotonous regularity.' Well that's too grandiose. A muddy patch is more my style. Concentrate on your women or they'll disappear. I'll send you some new poems as soon as I get them xeroxed.

Love, Love (that at any rate is true)

A neighbour drops in. She burbles on about corruption in the government, the high price of vegetables. Vera who is over for the evening fidgets through this conversation.

Dangerlok

You know, the neighbour says finally coming to the point, your bai works for me as well?

Yes.

I just wanted to warn you. That day I went into the kitchen and saw her helping herself to tea leaves, which she wrapped up and tucked into her sari.

Oh!

I didn't say anything. After all we need them.

Vera says irritably, Atleast she's not trying to murder us. Have you read about all those murders of women living alone or at home alone?

The neighbour is offended. I am telling you for your sake, she says.

I appreciate it, she says, but I've never known the bai to do anything like that.

Not the bai. She'd once had a young woman working for her who always helped herself to anything she wanted from the fridge. She had tried saying to her, Please ask me for anything you want. Don't just help yourself. But the girl had preferred to pinch the stuff. Maybe it tasted better that way. Anyway, it was no big deal.

Would you like some coffee, she says to the neighbour. Vera gives her a dark look. When the neighbour leaves Vera says, I'm surprised that servants don't murder more of these women.

The bai had once told her about a woman who was paying her about sixty rupees a month. On the days the woman was away and there was no work, she would cut the bai's pay.

A parent comes to the staffroom one day to tell her that their daughter will not be able to attend lectures for a while. She has developed a severe infection because of the contact lens she wears.

Barely two or three weeks later she sees the student going up the stairs to the lecture rooms, being led by a friend of hers. What on earth are you doing in college, she says, shouldn't you be resting? The girl's eyes look as opaque as those of someone who is blind.

The Principal told me that if I missed too many classes I would lose a year. So I've decided to come.

She is outraged when she hears this and goes to see the Principal. The student has been regular all through her first year, she says. How can you ask her to attend classes? She can't see a thing.

She can hear, can't she, says the Principal. If I let her get away with it what will the others think?

But she's not getting away with it. She's so stressed out already.

But it's no use. Rome hath spoken.

She decides it's time to go to the Sea Lounge, one of her favourite places, which she hasn't been to for a long time. She and Megan used to sit there, looking out at the bay. Later she and David used to go there and chat for hours over cups of coffee. Coffee used to be four rupees a cup when she and Megan went there. Now it's closer to forty.

There are no yachts in the bay now because of the rains. She looks at the heavy grey swell of the sea. On a clear day one can see all the way across to the other end of the bay. It's always difficult to remember that she is on the islands looking out to the mainland.

Vera's flat overlooks the bay, and that is one thing she envies her. They had once stood on the balcony watching a strange cloud looking like a seven-headed cobra bringing the rains across the bay. It had poured and poured, till the street looked like a river.

Many of the beautiful old bungalows had gone over the years, to be replaced by high-rise buildings at impossible prices. The most expensive slum in the world, someone had called Bombay. Stung, some of the citizens of the area had got together and created the Colaba Woods, a patch of green and trees where people came to jog, or sit around. Cars and taxis whiz by spewing exhaust, but for some strange reason, smoking is not allowed.

She used to enjoy exploring bits of Bombay she did

not know, restaurants that were not fashionable. But the glossies had changed all that. Columns on food had led to a rush of yuppies to ordinary places serving fish curry and rice, curried crab. Thrilled, the owners had refurbished their little places, so no more Rice Plate is Ready. Crab now appeared on the menu without a price, allowing the owners to charge whatever they wanted according to the season. Clerks and ordinary office staff stopped going to these places.

Dear David,

Thanks for your lovely long call. It must have cost you a bomb. Yes, I was hurt a bit but couldn't have come to the States anyway as there's no one to look after the parrots. I bought them without thinking about what it would involve. Story of my life. Yes of course I know you feel pleasing your girlfriends comes before everything else. We've been through that one several times! Don't try educating her for goodness sake. It was okay telling me things. At least I was willing to learn!

The parrots are yelling for attention so I've got to go. I've got commitments too! I can't tell you how hassly the mornings are. I wake up with the parrots at sunrise when they start yowling and go to the kitchen to make some tea. As soon as I enter a crow turns up at the window and starts cawing. I've given him things a couple of times and now he is very persistent. He likes cheese so I buy cheese especially for him. Vera says I've spoilt everyone including you and the crow.

Love Love and really it's all right.

The weather is a little warmer now, and the parrots decide they want a bath. Not the younger one, who faffs around in the bowl of water she puts out for them exactly at the same time every day. The other sits on the plate rack and spreads his wings. This means she has to splash water on them, that's the way he wants it. Parrotty cries of delight as she does so. Then he flies off, shakes off the water and comes back for more. Soon the kitchen is a mess, with water all over the wall and the floor. The bai, she knows, will have a fit.

Everyone says, Do the parrots talk? No, they don't. In Crawford Market, a parrot which can say Mittu sells for Rs 2,000. As if they had been to Harvard. But she usually knows what they are saying. If they want attention, they will try to pull off her glasses. If they don't want her to talk on the phone, they will chew the phone. She likes watching them when she gives them a nut or a bit of a biscuit. They curve their claws around it, but keep one claw crooked, like genteel ladies.

The only good thing to be said for the warm, muggy weather is the ice-cold watermelon juice. Full Glass Rs 6, Hap Rs 3. And the trees that flower in the summer, the flame of the forest, the cassias with their froth of pink blossom. There is nothing to be said for the first beads of sweat that begin to appear on her lip, and the spreading patches of damp that appear on everyone's shirts and cholis.

And the projects to be marked and exam papers in a steady tepid stream.

Asked to write an essay on the Stream of Consciousness Novel some poor lamb writes on the consciousness of streams. Eliot's *Fisher King* turns into a kingfisher. There's a poet lurking there in the backwoods, she thinks, but has to fail him. He is/she is not one of her students, just one of a mass from all over the state grinding through their BA Finals.

It's one of the mysteries of her world. Why do students who cannot write a single sentence in English major in

Eng Lit? Her own students can just about cope with Ros and Guil, and they are the privileged ones. She must ask the cynics. They'll know.

The sun is blazing as she gets off the bus. Stray dogs are napping under parked cars. They are washing down the tiles of the roadside shrine, and sparrows are frisking about in the pools of water that collect in the dips on the road.

The chemist's assistant can now sit down and watch the world go by. Utter walks through the gate with two kilos of vegetables in each hand.

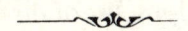

Scaffolding starts going up on many buildings in the lane. They must plaster and paint before the rains. Queen's Diamonds has not been plastered or painted for fifteen years. Everyone says the building will come down one of these days. But what to do with secretaries who buy themselves Maruti cars. The fourth floor flats leak so much, kitchen cupboards are warped and the walls streaked. The upstairs loo leaks into hers and the paint is peeling. The occupants refuse to let her plumber in. They have spent oodles on new and fancy tiles and they are not about to allow anyone to touch a single one.

The upstairs people are a pain in the neck. The son is good looking and with looks and new money the world is his kebab. He backs his Tata Sumo into the garden, breaking the bricks that form the border. She mentions it to his mother. The mother looks the other way when she passes her. What with the parrots and the upstairs people, her flat is a slum.

Another of those days, she thinks. The mother of a student who has shown up in class twice since the beginning of the academic year turns up to plead her case. She mentions a long list of dire illnesses that have afflicted the family; kidney transplants, cancer, and a great many others. The mother says the girl is really a good child, a mother's heart always knows.

Rina wonders why people in the wrong always lapse into Hindi film dialogue.

Have sympathy for me, at least, says the mother, and then adds briskly that the girl is planning to go to the States, should she postpone it if she may not be able to appear for her finals.

I don't know, she says. It's your decision.

Dangerlok

Walk, her doctor says.

Where? she asks. The roads are like choppy seas. If the municipality is not digging up the lane for cables and pipes, the telephone people are digging it up for cables. The bus tries to manouevre, and the left wheel goes into a ditch.

No bus, people tell each other forlornly. They have to walk to the end of the lane till the digging is over, if it is ever over.

The broken gutter which had been repaired is now broken again.

The Bombay Olympics, a cartoonist had called it. Leaping over ditches to get into a bus, hoiking up sarees to take a running leap into a train, leaping sideways to get out of the way of taxis that refuse to recognize pedestrain crossings.

Still, she thinks, I could never live anywhere else.

It seems to be the silly season. She has a number of strange calls, and can't think how these people got her number. To begin with there was someone who claimed to be an old student of the college, who was now into persuading people to grow mushrooms at home. Then there was the offer from a five star hotel for a Diners card plus of course a massive deposit.

Then came someone who mumbled the name of his company and said she had won a prize.

A prize? I haven't entered anything.

Your name came up with your telephone number in a draw.

Oh! What is this prize?

A water cooler or a casserole dish.

She had no use for either but said, Okay, just send someone here with it. I'm home after four.

No madam, we can't send anyone with it.

Why not?

You have to come here with your spouse.

With my spouse? I haven't got one.

Then you can't get the prize.

What nonsense! What's a spouse got to do with it?

That's the rule, madam.

So she knows what to say for the next call, this time from a newspaper. Madam, the festival season is beginning. If you are a Hindu, what do you want for Diwali and Dussera? If you're a Christian, what do you want from Santa Claus?

A man! A man! she said, and banged the phone down.

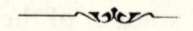

A rabid gentleman writes to the papers to say the city is going to the dogs. Apparently there are so many stray dogs that they will soon outnumber people, and people will have to flee or be hunted down by packs. They should all be poisoned or put to death some other way.

A Sunday supplement has a full colour page on gifts one can give. A pen studded with diamonds that costs a lakh. A tiara similarly studded. Lists of the sexiest people. Lists of the theme parties the sexiest are going to throw.

In the middle of the jumble the rising stars. She notices a picture of a girl who had wanted to major in English but hadn't been permitted to because she had not attended a single lecture for a year. She is proudly holding a book she has published. 'I wanted to do English,' she is quoted as saying, 'but my teacher said anyone who runs round trees as you do in your serials can't do English. I showed her my poems but she said I couldn't write.'

Well, well, well.

Goodness! It looks as if the gods themselves are descending in a machine to solve all problems:

> 'As Lara, Priyanka and Diya descended onstage in a magnificient boom crane amidst fireworks, son-of-the-soil Sukhbir followed it up with his foot-tappable "Girls, girls, most beautiful girls in the whole

world". And then, it was time for the final coutdown.'

You've missed the boat, Rina thinks, mixing her metaphors, we've gone down the drain years ago.

Dear David,

Thought I'd take a break and went to Poona with Vera who was going on some work. Ghastly journey. There wasn't a single second when there was quiet—hawkers, beggars, biscuits, chocolates, tea, coffee, newspapers, magazines, rulers, toys, vadas, omlette, sandwiches. Blind beggars, dozens of them, lame beggars, one with a foot growing out of his shoulder. I've been sleeping it off since I got back, can't bear the thought of going out for anything. I thought I was immune to noise and dirt, but this was really something.

Vera wanted to see some shops in the cantonment area but she couldn't find a single place to park, it was amazing. So I sat in the car while she looked at the shops. I went in briefly to Manneys where I had bought my very first book, *David Copperfield*, for Rs 4. Someone had given me Rs 5 for my birthday. Those were the days.

Dangerlok

Will write again when I'm less frazzled.
Love

She stands virtuously in a bus queue with her Rs 2.50 in her hand. It's a new bus driver, and she worries a little about the ones she was used to. Maybe they've gone on very long vacation to recover. But there's a seat vacant at the very front and she moves to it fast, before some schoolboy can grab it.

She has things on her mind and doesn't really notice where they are going till the bus stops on the bridge. There's a courtesy river under the bridge. The only time she has ever seen the water move is after a few weeks of rain. Then it goes back to its semi-solid state. But there's a spanking new flyover to compensate, and the signal time now is barely half a minute. Wow, it was painless today. She might even take the bus again. She picks up a few of the cheaper ballpoint pens for the parrots to wreck, and is on her way.

Great excitement in the Ladies Compartment First Class. Miss India has won some international award. She doesn't know whether these are cattle shows or not, she's never been to one or even watched it on TV. But anyone willing to live on carrot juice for a year certainly deserved an award. Wish they'd cut out the humbug, though. Between glitzy stints she is going to save widows and orphans.

Indian Women have Got What it Takes, says a headline in her neighbour's paper. Well some women have always had what it takes. Her bai is worth a dozen of the lazy sod she has married. And he has certainly pummelled her into shape.

And Utter has what it takes though she looks like a buffalo and behaves like one. And her aunt who is eighty-three has what it takes, because she still loves company and bright colours and jewellery and continued to wear her finery even after her husband died. And the kept woman glimpsed reading the stocks and shares page with a mobile phone in her hand has what it takes.

Mr Chopra who objected to the kept woman does not have what it takes, but the bus-driver has. He's had a coronary but who wouldn't, driving past Queen's Diamonds, and getting stuck at the corner ten times a day, while grinning rickshaw-wallas finish their tea and then amble out to move their vehicles to give the bus a little room.

The taxi driver who takes her from the college to Grant Road Station that day is not so sure.

Do you teach in this college? he asks. Yes, she says.

Have you seen all those college girls standing near the gate and smoking? he asks.

She is glad she hasn't lit a cigarette as she usually does. Just a few of them, she says.

Oh no, he says. I was the Vice Chancellor's driver for six years before I got this taxi and I've been to most of the colleges in Bombay. Everywhere the girls are smoking.

Oh!

Our Indian culture is going, he says, all spoilt by the West. Soon these girls will be divorcing their husbands. In the West they are always divorcing.

Don't women in the villages smoke bidis? she says.

That is altogether different, he says. Here they are seeing too many Western films. Our culture is going, all smoking and divorcing.

How can she console him?

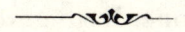

It's another one of those times. A colleague in Rina's department has invited a priest to give a lecture to her class. While her colleague goes to the canteen for some cups of coffee, the priest asks her where she lives. She tells him. Then she says, Some mornings I just sit around trying to decide whether I really want to go to college. I just can't face that bus-train-bus business.

The priest looks at her a moment and says, Don't you have any sense of responsibility for your students?

She would like to kick his shins. No, she says, I don't.

Vera doesn't help later by telling her she had dropped in on someone and mentioned the parrots and how amusing they were. And the person didn't let up after that about how wicked it was to keep pets in cages, and though Vera said they were not in cages, the woman wouldn't listen, and just went on and on. I tried my best, Vera says.

Don't bother, she says, that woman isn't the first to try to make me feel guilty. I can't do anything about them.

The parrots have started developing temperaments. The older one who is male does not like her to talk on the phone. He gives her a minute then jumps on her head and starts trying to chew the ear-piece or squawks into the phone. In the evenings, both want to be fed one sunflower seed at a time. And there must be a change of diet or they fling the stuff aside. Four to six is their quality time.

One day she is talking on the phone and it is very hot and without thinking she puts on the fan, she's forgotten the parrots are flying around. Suddenly there is a terrible thwack and she thinks oh my god and yells I can't talk now into the phone, puts off the fan and rushes to the corner where the bird has fallen. He is standing there with his eyes closed. She picks him up and talks to him and strokes his feathers gently, he is not hurt but he is in shock. For a while he opens his eyes and then closes them again. After a while he flies off but she watches him. Maybe he's concussed and he'll suddenly fall down dead. He does not. It's a miracle.

She wonders how long it will take someone to analyse why she has bought herself parrots. She has already been subjected to analyses of why she smokes. She was weaned too early. She misses oral pleasures. It is a short step from the lack of oral pleasures to the lack of a man, and so she is not surprised when some old student says apropos the parrots that she is glad her teacher has someone to look after. She is livid for an entire evening after the remark, which probably proves all the theories right.

Same saga, different names, says Vera.

Swine, says Rina who then proceeds to remind Vera of her own weird admirers: an ancient uncle who tried pushing her into a corner to kiss her, and a naïve young fellow who gave her some after-shave thinking it was perfume.

Swine, says Vera, and they decide to go off to a new Thai restaurant to forget their sagas old and new.

Jay rang last night, Rina says. He talked for twenty minutes about his cold.

It can't be that bad, Vera says, he's coming to a film with Mulk and me tonight.

Oh well, I made the required noises. What film is it?

I can't remember. Mulk felt like a film so he's bought some tickets. Do you feel like coming along?

No. I'd rather loll about at home.

Don't mope.

Of course not. My moping days are over.

The lazy Indian, she reads, perpetually lounging in inertia is a British concept. The Indian is a busy person. Through the heat of summer, the shiver of winter, the deluge of the monsoon, the moonlit nights of autumn, and the intoxication of our brief spring he has always much to do—a power-cut to survive, a bribe to give, a graft to take, an eve to tease, a wife to burn, a shradha to perform, a wedding to attend, a temple to visit, a vote to cast, a reputation to spoil, a government to criticize, a boot to deflect. Where, then, is the time to go under?

She recalls with amusement what a friend in Paris once told her. After a half-hour power cut, the friend he was living with called the minister to complain.

Don't waste your money, David says, I'll ring you back.

Telephone rates have come down, Rina says.

Never mind, he says. Put that phone down.

Sometimes she rings Megan, another old student who also lives abroad. Megan is one of her failures, not as a student, no, she was one of the most intuitive in her class. But she burdened Megan with her depressions and did not notice what Megan felt about anything. Sometimes they'd go to a film together, or a play or an exhibition but one day Megan cut loose. It was no surprise but a great grief to her. Megan was the first woman she could talk to about anything.

There's a story in college, Megan had once said, that you were ditched at the altar in your wedding dress, and she was amazed and said but it could not have been a dress and it would not have been an altar, so where did that story come from?

Students who knew Megan used her as a hotline for information about their teacher who, intriguingly, was not married. Did she wear nighties, one of them asked Megan. Did she do normal things like going out for dinner, or just chatting with friends?

Dear David,

I'm sorry I was half asleep when you rang and couldn't say anything much, but I suppose you didn't really want any comments anyway. I thought when I hadn't heard from you that you were busy. Didn't think it was a crisis.

It's been a tiring week at college. Some bureaucratic bozos came to assess the college. They reeked of Delhi with all their talk of do we give the students certificates and the rest. I said we encouraged our students not to work for certificates for every little thing, and one of the guys said, Human Nature being such, an Ordinary Man Will Not Be Impressed if his child has published an Article in an Academic Journal. He will be Impressed by a Certificate.

Taxi fares are going up again. The guy at the corner whose taxi I often use says he'll charge me the old rates but I am not to tell the other drivers. My mother's brother who is in England sent me some money so I've been doing some quick calculations on how much I can afford by way of zooming about.

Take care.
Love, Love

Dear David,

So you may come back for a year just to take a break before completing your Ph.D? How wonderful. I'm really thrilled. And the girlfriend is coming back too? I thought she was an American citizen.

The girlfriend is a younger version of me? Good grief. The younger version of me was a mess!

Anil was here recently. He's at a small college near San Francisco and likes it but would like to move to a city. He asked for news of you. He brought me a carton of Camel Lights, which took some getting used to, and Ginger Fish. The small print calls it a ginger ale scented fish. Lemon and lime intertwine with the effervescent spiciness of ginger. I think I'll try it when I don't have to go to college!

Love

She gets into a cab downtown and the driver says, How is your little dog?

Amazing, in a city of fifty-five thousand taxis.

Don't you remember, he says, I drove you to the clinic with the pup.

He died.

I'm sorry, the driver says. I wish you hadn't taken

him to a municipal clinic. They don't look after them.

I made a mistake. I shouldn't have told them he was a stray. A friend of mine who took his own dog there said they were very good to him.

I wish you had gone to the doctor I recommended.

She asks his name, and he tells her he lives on her road.

It's a comforting feeling, knowing so many people who live in her area. She can't imagine living anywhere else in India, let alone abroad.

It has been pouring, unseasonal summer rain. The bai says water has been entering the room and the roof is leaking. She tells the bai to come to her flat for the night till the problem is over.

The bai giggles. My husband will kill me, she says. Why?

The bai gives her a sidelong look. Should she say what she is going to say to a woman who is single? My husband wants sex every night, she says.

Why don't you tell him you're tired? You work all day.

I've told him so many times. But he doesn't work so he has lots of energy.

Oh!

Dangerlok

You're so lucky not to be married. It's a big nuisance, marriage, the bai says.

Mm!

My neighbour has a smaller room than mine, the bai says, so two of her children sleep under the bed. One day the little boy said to his grandmother, Aji, in the night the bed goes dhap dhap. I get frightened.

What did the grandmother say?

The bai giggles again. What can she say? She said go wash your face and do your lessons.

As the taxi stops at the traffic lights, she watches the two women cast a quick glance around. If there are Arabs in any of the cabs or cars, the two make a quick dash to them.

We have a corpse to bury.

When there are no Arabs, the locals will have to do.

We have a corpse to bury and no money for the funeral.

What happened, she asks, to the corpse you had yesterday, and the day before?

They walk away.

She can't even stand the sight of them.

Mr Chopra who lives on the floor below, next to the kept woman, is of the opinion that servants should be treated as servants, otherwise they sit on your head. He has many stories in this repertoire. Mrs So-and-So only paid her servant so much and the servant worked for years. Mrs XYZ insisted that the servant do a full two hours of work whether there was work or not. If there wasn't much, she created some. And the servant stayed with her for years.

Plus, he says, they only work for one hour or a little more, they work in three-four houses, they make lots of money.

She has heard this sort of thing from so many people she does not know whether it is worth commenting on. But still she says, If they don't come for one day, we're lost. We can't manage without them. And the work they do is hard work.

But, he says, that is their work, as if they were born to it, which in a way they were.

She says, But that is only because they don't have the chance to do anything else. My bai, she adds, wants her daughters to go to school and learn something so they get a different kind of job.

You go look in their homes, they have televisions and radios, he says.

She says, The shops will close if I don't leave immediately.

Dangerlok

Whatever you do, don't write about me, says Jay.

It's the only way Jane Austen could cope with the people she lived with, says Rina.

I don't give a damn about Jane Austen, says Jay.

Mulk isn't worried that I'll write about him, says Rina.

What can one write about Mulk in any case, says Jay.

I'll tell him you said that.

Oh God! It's not my evening. Why can't you stick to parrots?

Well, I've finished writing about parrots. Now I want to write about people. I won't say you have a bald spot. David says I can write anything about him. In fact he says I should make it nasty or no one will believe me.

David's in New York. He's safe.

You choose your women badly Jay, Rina says.

Jay's shit scared, said Vera. What did you say to him?

I told him writing was the weapon of the weak and the vulnerable.

I'm sure he loved that.

I told him I wouldn't write about his bald spot.

He asked me to talk to you, said Vera.

Ha! said Rina.

Dear David,

Only six months to go! I hope...

No, she wouldn't offer him a room in her flat. It was too disorienting. Once, long ago, he had asked if he could bring a girlfriend there, and she had said okay, and stayed over at Vera's. But now she wouldn't. She had given up trying to be high-minded and generous. She wanted peace.

She tore up the page and started again.

Dear David,

But she didn't seem to be able to burble on any longer. She tore up the page.

Dear David,

Do you remember I told you ages ago the English Board of Studies was in trouble because of some allegedly obscene poems included in the syllabus? Well, that's finally been solved. I remembered someone who knew someone sensible in the police and it was sorted out. Now the Board members actually smile at me.

Really, Eng Lit departments are held to account for all kinds of things these days, including the decline of civilization. One of these Delhi prattlers has even said in writing that Eng Lit teachers think that the so-called sanctity of literature puts us above such mundane things as rises in bus fares and bureaucratic interference in education. They are really crazy. The first teacher's union secretary was a poet!

Love

Dear David,

I've written a different kind of poem from the parroty ones so I'm not sure it works. Let me know. By the way, the you in the poem isn't you:

I want a father;
Always have.
God won't do.
He's too judgemental.
And so I found you...
Like my father, absent.

Another one I've abandoned. Too slick:

> There's something to be said
> For suffering.
> It improves your lectures on tragedy quite
>   remarkably.

Rina is curious when she receives a letter in handwriting she does not recognize. It turns out to be the author of a book she had reviewed unfavourably. The letter is two pages of personal abuse, a nice way of avoiding answers to the points she had raised. She is called a snake, an enemy of women, an anti-post-colonialist, a would-be F. R. Leavis, pompous, hysterical, aging. Mrs Gandhi was assassinated but who was going to take care of her? She should stop writing because she was aging and looked after parrots, in any case she had achieved nothing, certainly nothing compared to the author who was a full professor while she was a mere lecturer (not true), and he had contributed far more to the welfare of humankind than she could ever hope to do. It was pathetic to see a woman her age running after publishers with her one-line thingies, which she thought were poetry.

Dangerlok

She shows the letter to Vera. Vera says, who does he think you should run after if you want to publish? The grocer?

Well, said Rina, it may come to that. I'll have to sell the stuff as wrapping paper and then when people buy their little packets of rice or daal they get a poem to read as well.

It is a relief really to have sourly sensible friends like Vera.

Mrs D'Costa has a picture of Christ on her front door. Most people have a holy picture or tile on the front door or on the wall near the front door. Ganesh is the most popular.

Someone has spat betel juice on her picture of Christ. She is angry and bewildered. Is it because she does not allow her daughters to mix with the local yokels? She used to live in one room in a chawl. Now that the children were growing up, she wanted them to have a place they could bring their friends to. Her husband was in the Gulf.

A friend in the chawl told Mrs D'Costa he knew a local don. The don liked to do favours, personal favours, and impersonal ones. He came riding pillion, with a heavy gold chain, and a heavier moustache.

Utter's son came on behalf of persons unnamed to apologize for the incident. But Mrs D'Costa is no longer at ease.

Rina has a fever. For a few days, its slow burning will keep her conscious of nothing but itself. She brews some tea, lights a cigarette. Snap.

When she bought her flat, Rina hadn't realized they were so close to the airport. She had to say just a minute on the phone several times a day as the planes zoomed by her windows. The smaller they were the more noise they made. She had asked the agent about noise. Plenty of noise, he had said with satisfaction. She had looked at him uncertainly, not sure that he had understood the question which she had asked in English. Well, she had thought, she wouldn't have to pay a fortune to and from the airport. But the taxi drivers were sullen about short distances and swore when she refused to give them twice the fare. An extra fiver maybe or a tenner as a peace offering. They would drive off in contempt, flinging the note on the pavement.

All dangerlok, the bai would say, and proceed to tell her stories of the iniquites of taxi drivers and the world in general, and the inhabitants of Queen's Diamonds in particular.

Still, it was nice to be in one's own flat with one's own bits of furniture. When she had first come to Bombay she was a paying guest, first with a Parsi lady who was used to Christians, and then with a Sindhi lady who was not. Or at least the friends of the Sindhi lady were not. Her little room had no window, just a couple of slats in the door, which opened into the main flat. When the landlady was away the friends would question the maid. Has the Christian been fed? one of them used to ask. The landlady was more discreet. Why do you wear these cotton saris? she would say. Let me give you one of these nylon ones I no longer use. Rina would smile and say no, thank you, really.

Still it was because of the landlady that she now had a flat of her own. We are business people, the landlady would say. We know that prices are going up. In six months you will never again be able to afford a flat. Beg, borrow. I will ask my brothers to show you places you can afford. In those days even Rs 35,000 was an impossible sum. What could she save on a salary of Rs 585 a month?

The building was called Queen's Diamonds. Good grief. How on earth would she tell her friends she lived in something with a name like that. Not that there was much choice in the area. The others were Silver Streak, Gold Bangles and worse. Forget the tired irony of the garbage heap at the gate, and the broken, open gutters choked with thin blue and pink plastic bags.

A redevelopment of what used to be a chawl? her mother had said when she rang her. What sort of people will you have for neighbours? Well, now she knew.

Thinking of the abusive letter she had received, Rina wonders how the person who wrote it, a person she barely knows, knew that she was attempting to write poems, and that she kept parrots. There were only two or three people she had told these things, and they were friends. Well, friends told their friends who are not necessarily one's own friends or even acquaintances and so it went. Really, Utter (that old buffalo Mrs D'Costa of the Chirst picture calls her) gossiping under the almond tree with another old buffalo seems small cheese by comparison. At least she didn't get to know what they gossiped about, didn't feel an invasion of her privacy.

My God, thinks Rina, even those stupid glossies that

arrive every day with the newspaper, full of party animals and starlets and people who give theme parties, seem harmless compared with what is happening in the media. She doesn't have a computer, but friends ring occasionally with bits of the Internet. At least one such carries assessments of the work of writers followed by confident assessments of and judgements on the private lives or what are alleged to be the private lives of the writers. All summed in one or two paras. One would have sued the print media for some of the stuff, if one had the money, but one never did.

It's a strange new world that hath such people in it. She's beginning to feel like a dinosaur.

There's only one solution for all problems: a cup of tea. She takes down the tea leaves and the sugar, bungs in some milk and water and brews a mugful. She lights a cigarette. A light breeze blows the smoke back into the room. There are already brown patches on the ceiling. The place is a slum.

I'll go to Elephanta, she thinks, and wonders if Vera would like to come along. There's a boat every hour or so. She will climb the hill, fend off vendors of mineral water filled at the nearest tap, candy floss, cornelian necklaces. She will tut tut about the Portuguese who use the stone carving inside the cave for target practice.

She will sit on a bench and watch the monkeys

investigate discarded cartons. And she will soak in the wide grey, sea.

Dear David,

The students have decided they want to do *Macbeth* for our festival this year, and they've found a place to do it in. Do you remember all those derelict mills in Central Bombay? Well, they are now full of art galleries, pool parlours, leisure centres, and restaurants where the sandwiches cost more than the tickets for our plays. There's a shed right on top of one of the buildings full of all kinds of detritus. The students are going to pile the stuff together in interesting ways (found sculpture) to suggest a devastated landscape on the way to the stage area. Some of the students however are not sure we should use the place because of all the textile workers who lost their jobs. It is strange to see glitzy expensive new apartment blocks coming up in the mill area. They don't want to call it Lower Parel any more because it sounds too lower class. I think it's called Worli East!

Well, we at Queen's Diamonds are going up in the world too. The bai was very excited because some minor TV star has moved in, at least I think she's minor, I've never heard of her!

Another instalment coming up soon, hopefully less morose. Do you want the *Where to Eat Guide*, which has just come out, as a present?

Love

Dear David,

So you're coming alone but with orders not to stay with me? I hope I'll get a hug at least.

I had lunch with your mother yesterday. She said she wished you wouldn't change your girlfriends as often as you change your socks! I told her you would always change your girlfriends as often as you would change your socks. She misses the happily ever after. Don't we all?

It will be nice to know you are around anyway. Only a while to go. Can you get me some Raymond Chandlers? I don't seem to be able to find any here, not even at the pavement shops.

Love, Love

One couldn't even go to the Himalayas. They were

full of admen and their gurus. One couldn't go back to Nature. Nature was mosquitoes. And resorts, hotels, shops, industries all the way to the hill-stations near Bombay. And incessant traffic. Nor is there any sign of the rain. The city is sulphurous. The day-long downpour didn't cool the place two weeks ago, merely disrupted the railways, roadways, telephones. The same old pictures appeared in the papers of localities that looked like lakes. Rina can't believe that year after year some intrepid reporter actually wades in knee-deep water to take those pictures.

The rains have gone away, the taxi driver says.

Looks like it, she says, wondering why he is driving as if he wants her to take in the view.

The rains, and then the slow slide to Christmas. Uncle John was always the first to arrive. She would look at him adoringly and he would pick her up and lift her over his head. And cousin Ivor was so beautiful, even she knew that. For him she would sing I see the moon and the moon sees me.

Jay?
 Hi.
 What's that noise in the background?

Stir-fry.
Ouch.
Ouch is right. It's the bai's evening off.
Shall I ring you back?
Don't ring me. I'll ring you.
Okay beastie, enjoy.

The thing to do, Vera said, is to make one of those plus and minus charts. You know, David high cheekbones, low morals; Jay no cheekbones, no morals. David disloyal bastard, Jay not worth being loyal to. David sexy? she said giving Rina a sharp look. Rina hated discussing 'these things' as she called them.

Sexy.

Let's toss a coin, Vera said. She threw the coin into the air and caught it as it fell. On second thoughts, she said, let's have a drink instead.

It was a long time before the sound of the phone registered. Oh dear, Rina thought. She could never remember these late night conversations in the mornings.

You're half asleep and I'm half drunk, said David. But I called to say I miss you. I even fantasize about you.

Rina turned on the bedside lamp and looked at herself in the mirror. With her faded nightie and her hair dry and sticking up all over the place she decided she was not exactly worth fantasizing about.

Too complicated, Rina said.

What's too complicated, David said. You know I love you. The rest are just forays.

David, she said. David.

IBH/02510/11/04